Fires at Christmas

E. R. Kaye

0

1

Chapter One

"God, I hate flying." Julie muttered, clenching her fists in her lap, her entire body tense. She winced as turbulence grabbed the wings of the airbus that had been the only last minute option left to her. A business class option on a tiny jet meant no in-flight service, no pillow or blanket, and certainly no leg room. She'd crammed her purse into the carryon, or she would still be in Chicago, sleeping in the terminal of O'Hare, so she didn't have access to the things she really wanted. Like chapstick. The tired flight attendant was not sympathetic about the one bag rule, and Julie wasn't interested in checking her suitcase. She wanted to get home, but she had regretted her hasty impulse every moment of the bumpy flight on the puddle jumper. The last several hours had been a miserable, tortured mess, and the woman to her left smelled like cheese.

Julie was heading home to Christmas together with her husband, hoping that he was ready to make this marriage work. She knew he wasn't perfect, but she also kept hoping that he would come around. They had once been wildly in love. Last week, before she left, he had even mentioned the idea of kids. That had to be a sign. She had momentarily considered it.

Julie imagined what kids with her husband would look like. Their faces were blurred, but she could see them as dark haired and—short. Her smile turned to a grimace, and she gazed at the wedding ring with the antique cut surrounding a giant diamond that fit her left hand, remembering her wedding day. Adam was only about two inches taller than she was. He wouldn't even let her wear heels at their wedding. She had settled for flat sandals. Every one of her pictures with him had been with her sitting down. Kids with him meant a lifetime of staving off his little-man-insecurity fears.

"I better get a handle on this attitude," she sighed softly. "I want this to work. I want this to work. He is the love of my life. We are good together." The woman next to her turned her head in Julie's direction and she pinched her mouth shut. She felt like a fraud. Adam had rescued her in a moment of sadness and he'd lorded it over her ever since.

The pilot spoke over the intercom to say the weather in Amarillo was bright and the air was perfect for an easy landing. It seemed last night's storm was long in the past, but the bump of turbulence at that moment gave his words a hint of a lie. Julie swallowed hard and imagined seeing Adam earlier than expected. He was going to be surprised, but she felt confident that the negligee she was wearing beneath her sweater would go a long way in helping get them back on the right track. Sex had always been one thing they were good at.

She stepped off the plane, her jaw clenched in a plastic smile as she moved into the terminal. Almost home. Her suitcase stopped short and hauled her backwards a half step, her scarf tangled in the wheels.

The smile wavered slightly as she quickly wrapped her mother's handmade blue and white keepsake around her neck instead, and then pulled her jacket over her shoulders. Her wedding ring flashed as she hauled her wheeled carryon through the terminal past the bank of windows and toward the parking garage exit.

Finishing early in Chicago meant an early flight home. She remembered the early days of their marriage when Adam would grab her in his arms with a wicked laugh and call her his little love. She missed the easy days of courtship before she realized how mean and inconsiderate he truly was. She had prepared herself for a sexy scene and hoped it would come to pass. He could still get her excited, and she wanted to feel alive in his arms again. Julie smiled in anticipation.

She could see it–the red wine she had stashed in the kitchen, the lacy camisole she now wore beneath her cashmere sweater, his hands on her hips. She licked her lips as she thought about how cozy the apartment would be, a trail of clothing left behind them.

"Oh Adam," she muttered, "please be thrilled to see me." The dread that welled up in her at the idea that had been festering in her heart threatened to spill over. "Please, God. Make him love me again." She felt useless. Worked over. Tired. If Adam didn't love her anymore, she wasn't sure how she was going to stand up tomorrow. Or the day after. Or what life would be like after failure in love. Since her parents had died, she had become a shell of who she had once been. She felt pathetic, even now, but the shadow of a backbone forced her to stand straight. "Suck it up, sister. You're tougher than this." She stepped off the curb and landed her heeled suede boot flat in a pile of slush.

"Great." She swiped a hand at the muck that now coated her favorite boots and almost lost her balance. "Ruined."

As she slipped into the parking garage, she glanced around her. *Thank God I parked in the garage, instead of out in that mess.* She found her car easily, sending up another prayer that she would make it home safely. The weather had been damp lately, and the cars left out in the open were gray with it. Fortunately, the old Sebring started faithfully and warmed quickly.

Life is grand. She sighed, hopeful that the rest of her day would go as well.

Thirty minutes later, Julie stepped into the downtown penthouse apartment that Adam had insisted on and heard voices.

What's Sara doing here?

The glamorous black leather purse casually dropped on the floor, the birthday scarf, the remodeled 80s tweed that could only belong to Sara, each gave Julie a shiver of dread. A giggle rang out flirtatiously and Julie moaned softly. "Why are you guys doing this to me?" Her agonized whisper poured over her lips as she moved closer to the bedroom and the voices that she loved, and her heart sank deeper and deeper in her chest.

She turned to leave, but stopped, suddenly furious. The doorknob seemed to glow red in front of her, the door itself shifted to a firey orange in the haze of fury she had always repressed, but which now exploded within her. She wanted to rip the door open and scream because she knew what lay behind it. Instead, she took a long, solid breath and slowly exhaled, the red fading to a pink. Only then did she open the door.

Cozily huddled in a sweet embrace—had it been two other people–in front of the blazing fireplace she had begged Adam for and that he refused to allow her to use, they sat. Naked.

The two turned to her and their jaws dropped. Sara scrambled to cover her breasts.

"Julie, I didn't think you were coming home until next week!" Adam jumped up and the tattoo on his hip flashed in the firelight. Bile rose in her throat and she coughed on the gag that choked her.

She watched as the scene played slowly out in front of her, Adam rushing toward her, Sara pulling Julie's favorite sherpa blanket around her naked chest and hips. She blinked and it sped up again, but she was suddenly deaf to Adam's pleas for her to wait.

She turned without a word and gently closed the door to the bedroom behind her. She heard Adam fumbling after her, but she calmly closed the front door behind her too. She was too ladylike to slam doors or to start crying or screaming at the two who had betrayed her. The anger was gone as quickly as it had come. She walked into the kitchen, clambered up on the chair, pulled the bottle of wine off the back of the refrigerator, and as she heard the bedroom door open, she calmly closed the front door behind her. The Sebring waited faithfully as she tossed her suitcase in, shut the trunk, and started driving.

Chapter Two

Snow glared off the headlights and tractor trailers pushed gusts of slush and sleet onto the windshield of Julie's five year old Sebring. She popped the wipers into higher mode and the "service engine light" blinked on.

"Not again," Julie groaned. She had noticed it coming on and off periodically since the day before, but hadn't had it checked as she drove across the state of New Mexico. Although the Chrysler shuddered when she accelerated at stop lights, it still ran and it wasn't making angry noises, so Julie kept on. This time, however, the light came on and the car began to shake as she moved her foot off the accelerator.

"Oh, no, no, no." Julie began to pull off to the side of the freeway when she noticed an exit sign ahead. "Great." While the car wouldn't accelerate, it did continue to coast along, the Edgewood exit crawling closer and closer. She noticed a Wal-Mart just off the highway and rolled the car into a parking space just inside the entry. She smacked her hand on the dash and slumped over the wheel. The engine happily wheezed to a stop and the car quit.

"What luck. Where in the world am I?" She looked around at the barren parking lot, a smattering of people in cars and trucks braving the weather to pick up items they probably didn't need. In the minute the car had been parked, large flakes had begun to cover it. Julie pulled her scarf around her neck a couple of times and zipped her jacket beneath the steering wheel.

"Food. At least there will be food." For the twentieth time that day she kicked herself for only packing a sandwich and a bag of almonds. She punched her shoulder at the door and climbed out of the coupe. The remote had broken a month or two before, so she pushed the lock with her finger and shut the door as a clump of slush hit the pavement under the front wheel.

Even with her heavy down jacket, the wind cut through her, buffeting her back against the car. Julie leaned into it, snowflakes driving into her face, and pushed toward the doors of the superstore. Her running shoes filled with slush and she felt her ankles chill over the short socks she wore. *Certainly prepared for winter,* she thought wryly. *Maybe next year, I'll fly to Miami instead.*

"Happy Holidays!" The greeter smiled at Julie as she stamped her feet under the overhead heaters.

"Right, to you too." In that exchange, she remembered for the umpteenth time why she felt the need to run this time of year, but especially this one. The holidays failed to hold a special place in her heart or her mind since her parents had died, but this one was a particularly torturous year. Adam's face lurked in the corner of her brain and she shook her head as if it would erase his face. *Bastard.* She thought. *Lying, cheating bastard.*

"Sure is snowing out there!" The greeter peered

around Julie at the snow reflecting off the parking lights. "Hope we can get out of here before it gets too bad."

Julie continued wiping her wet feet on the already soaked entry carpet, but looked up at the elderly woman with the faded dye in her hair, the drab brown sweater hanging on old shoulders that stooped under age. Momentarily she forgot how miserable she was and saw a woman who had once been beautiful sitting before her. Even through the obvious burden of years, the smile in the greeter's eyes gave her hope that happiness did exist. She felt her mood settle and she surrendered to the kindness of the older woman.

"Yes, it's sure starting to come down."

The greeter stood and moved toward the door. "I better call my Donny to come get me. I think it's time to call it a night." The greeter became distracted by the snow flurries that made it difficult to see beyond the light of the entryway. "They don't really want greeters to work too many hours anymore anyway."

Julie smiled vaguely at the innocent blathering and looked around to notice the largest store she had ever seen. There was a tiny McDonald's to her left and an extensive array of produce to her right. Just in front of her, a display of gloves, hats, and umbrellas brightly reminded her that the weather seemed to be getting worse since she had left Tucumcari that afternoon, as if the weather outside hadn't done enough to send that message. The snow shovels and ice melt formed a backdrop for all of this.

She sighed. It seemed Texas was a long way away,

though she had just left this morning on this new adventure alone. She felt the snowflakes drip onto her scalp through her long curls and thought about purchasing a hat, but instead she focused on the grumbling of her stomach. She slid her hand through her hair and thanked God she'd let it grow over the last year.

"Well, I guess I can get a burger...or maybe an apple." A McDonald's employee pulled the metal grate closed around the restaurant and locked the door. "Oh. I guess I'll go for the apple." She mumbled to herself, blinking wisps of moisture off her eyelashes and pulling her gloves off with her teeth.

"What's that honey?" The greeter was still peering out the window but turned to talk to Julie.

"Oh, nothing. I better get my shopping done so I can get out of here!" Right. As if she had anywhere to go, and not only that, but her car didn't sound like it was much in the mood for more travel. She might be camping out in the backseat, for all she knew. That promised to make for a very cold night. Good thing she had her mother's quilt in the backseat, as always.

Julie wandered through the produce and before long, found herself meandering through the store, taking in all of the merchandise prepped for Christmas. A display blinked the hours until the big day, reminding Julie that she only had a couple of days to buy presents for...no one. It seemed her life had been put on hold in the last month and she hadn't bought a Christmas gift for a single person since. Usually her shopping was done by Thanksgiving. Now, who did she have in her life to give gifts to? She definitely felt like a Grinch as she thought of her friend Hilary and her next door neighbor's son, Jayden. Nope, they weren't even getting a gift this year. She was in a decidedly stingy mood and didn't care who knew it.

She flipped through the videos in the bargain bin and continued wandering through the home section, thinking how nice it had been to have a home filled with love and contentment. Her new apartment in Amarillo waited for her, but it certainly wasn't filled with love. It was merely a place to sleep and shower. Her tiny space was a place her books resided, but not a place where Julie really felt at peace. The occasional movie at home was a lonely affair, and usually occurred only when she was ill. She missed the days when she and Adam would spend months watching Christmas movies together, enjoying quality time laughing at movies they had seen hundreds of times before. She just didn't miss them enough to take him up on his most recent request for her to come back home.

Home certainly was where the heart was, but she wasn't sure she even had a heart anymore.

"Oh well." She shrugged to no one in particular and headed toward the checkout, her load of apples and cheese sticks grasped firmly in her fist. *I suppose I should go see what I can do about my car.* She paid and headed out the door into a raging swirl of wind and snow. The drifting snowflakes had turned into a raging blizzard. *How did that happen so quickly?* She pushed toward her crippled vehicle, evading the growing drifts that were forming in the aisles. *I wasn't in there that long, was I?* She jabbed her key into the door lock and opened the door, just as a gust of wind grabbed a hold of the door and knocked her off balance. Her foot caught a patch of ice and she hit the pavement, her head bouncing off the curb, her apple rolling under the tire.

Chapter Three

Diego pulled his diesel farm truck into a parking space near the entrance of the shopping plaza and put it in park. The wiper blades scraped across the window, clearing the snow as quickly as it fell. He sat quietly, thinking about how quickly Christmas had come upon him. He was going through the motions these days, enjoying his family, but missing something that he couldn't quite put his finger on. He loved his family. His sister and her husband made wonderful friends, and their children were as special to him as if they were his own.

The aching loneliness of missing out on life pushed at him, his pores drinking it in like an old friend. Christmas. Again.

Alone. Again.

Diego wasn't desperate for the attention of women; he never had been. He'd had his share of that life. As a rodeo star, and especially a bullrider, he'd had his choice of women of all shapes and sizes, but now that he had retired, he was sure *she* had still never come into his life. He was sure she was still out there somewhere. The problem was he didn't have time to go look for her. He had a ranch to run and that kept him busy from sunup to sundown. In a lot of ways, he regretted that. His plan had always been to get married and settle down before he was 30. Nights out at the dancehall were fun, in a carefree kind of way, but lately the women had seemed superficial, insincere, and more interested in his fame than in his dreams. Not to mention that the last woman he'd dated had tried to kill him.

Patti had definitely been a wild ride. She was fast, gorgeous, and wanted to play a long-term role in his pants. He was convinced it was more that she liked his belt buckle. They had a name for girls like that, but Diego didn't realize she was a buckle bunny until she started taking and quit giving. He sucked in a breath at his foolish pride.

Last Christmas had been fun, though. Patti was a charmer. She'd weaseled her way into the lives of the kids pretty easily, and that had been hard to explain. Aidan still asked about her, and he was only a little kid.

"Gettin' old, cowboy."

Idly, he wiped the dust from the stereo window with his finger and watched a young woman battling the wind and the whirling snow, her hair whipping in the air behind her, the gusts of wind grabbing at the edges of her coat. Snow blustered against the woman while the wipers that still moved in a rhythmic motion on his windshield suddenly seemed to have a hard time keeping up. The snow was already piling up on the cars and on the parking lot. At the moment, Diego didn't envy the woman's slight height, cocooned inside an enormous down jacket.

He reached for his cowboy hat, zipped his jacket and shut down the truck, taking one last look out the windshield. It was hard to tell through the thickening snow, but it appeared the woman he had just been observing was on the ground, and she wasn't moving. "What the hell?" Without a second thought, he dropped everything and was out of his truck in a bound.

Chapter Four

Julie was lying in a puddle of slush at least an inch deep. She couldn't feel anything but the cold that was beginning to seep through her clothes; she moaned as she rolled onto her side and tried to put her feet under her. Her legs felt heavy and she wanted to vomit.

"Miss? Are you okay?" Someone was holding her head up.

"Don't you know you aren't supposed to move someone when they've been knocked out?" Julie grumpily moaned as the pain suddenly arced through the back of her head and the cold of the snow under her backside worked its way into her bones.

"If I didn't know better, I'd say that you are!" She heard his soft chuckle and felt the cool air hit her wet head when he released her head. A tangled strand of her hair was wrapped around his glove and as she pulled back his hand went with her. She put her hand up and grasped her hair and eyed him suspiciously. His sheepish expression made her relax. Snowflakes coated her face and she clumsily wiped them off with the back of her hand. She probably just smeared mud across her face for all she knew.

"Would you like a hand up?"

Despite herself, she liked what she saw. His eyes were dark in the night, ringed by darker lashes. Under the black cowboy hat and the brown canvas jacket, a very tall, very athletic man unfolded himself and stood above her. Julie tried to scramble to her feet, but only made it to her knees before she moaned and almost fell forward onto the man's boots. Some impression. She kicked herself for admiring him in this moment when she was such a wreck. Fortunately, her body distracted her at that moment.

"I—I think I am going to throw up." Awkwardly, she put her hand out to her car.

"Hang on, hang on, it's going to be okay. You took a nasty slip. Just sit here for a sec, and I'll help you up when you're ready." He leaned in with his hands, kneeling in front of her again, concern etched across his brow. She pulled her coat closed at the neck where the zipper had broken a month before.

"It's fr-freezing. I'm so cold."

"You're soaked, and it's snowing pretty hard. Do you have someone you can call?" He held her elbow as she regained her composure. "You might need to see a doctor."

"No, no, I'm okay. I just should go back inside, I guess."

"And sit where? And do what?" He gestured at the employees hovering at the door, ushering people out. "It looks like they are shutting this place down anyway." Julie moved toward the door of her car again and fumbled in her pockets for her keys, forgetting that

they were already in the door. "I'm fine. I'll be fine."
Blearily she looked around for her keys on the ground,
realizing they were missing from her hand. Tears
sprang to her eyes and she hastily wiped at them,
trying not to let the stranger see her fear.

"Hey," He said it gently, and she almost sobbed. "I
don't think you should be driving right now anyway."
He tapped lightly on the keys still hanging from the
door lock and they made a soft tinkle on the wind of the
blizzard. "I'll take you to Betty Lee's. Natalie and I can
take care of you until we can get Doc Langan out here."

Julie raised her chin in defiance, determined to solve
this one on her own. The last time she had trusted a
man when she was in duress, she'd married him, and
he had turned out to be the biggest mistake of her
lifetime. She wasn't making even remotely the same
mistakes twice. But this man was a strong temptation,
even in her clearly concussed condition.

"No, I'm okay, really. I'll just try to start the car--"
"Try to?"

Julie looked up, panicked. "Oh, no! My car quit a
minute ago and I'm not from here and..." anguish rang
loud and clear in her eyes as she processed how alone
she was in a strange town with him, a strange man. She
could just imagine what he was thinking. *She's an easy
target.* She hoped he wasn't thinking that. Some
cowboy was kneeling in front of her *and* her disabled
car and she could barely think past the pain in her
head. She had a knot the size of the apple he'd spied
under her tire. She prayed this man was truly a kind
man and not the kind she'd read about in so many

murder mysteries.

"Hey—you ok?" The man was gentle enough, but Julie couldn't tolerate his kindness in her weakness.

"No! I'm not okay! I'm stranded in some strange town, in a parking lot, and I have no idea what to do..." She clamped her mouth shut. She'd just told a perfect stranger how easy she was to murder and get away with it. She groaned and told herself *I have got to stop watching so much tv.*

To make matters worse, the stranger reached out a hand to steady her shoulder, clearly unnerved by her tears. She drew herself up and moved away from his simple gesture. She trembled as she climbed out of the wet puddle she had been lying in. Grace was denied her on this day, as she slipped again, succeeding in soaking the sleeves of her jacket up to her elbow as she braced herself with her hands. He leaned in to help her again, but she squared her shoulders and swallowed her tears, giving him a weak grin to show that she wasn't going to dissolve any further into a crying fit. He reached out a hand once again to steady her.

"I think I'm okay. My bigger dilemma is that I'm not sure my car is going to run. It quit on the freeway and I was lucky to make it to this parking lot." She grasped his hand and let him help her to a standing position. Her brain was screaming caution, but her body was just over the entire conversation. She needed some help. She wobbled uneasily and leaned on the door of her car. Stranger or not, he was gentle, and she needed that. She'd been denied human compassion for what seemed like an eternity.

18

Her head dropped into her hands as she realized she didn't have anywhere to go, and this man was offering his home and help. Betty Lee had to be his mother—or mother-in-law, and Natalie was probably his wife, with Julie's luck, but she was only vaguely concerned at the moment, as she thought she might fall over again. Maybe she should just take him up on the offer. Get it over with. Either embrace the help, or get murdered along the way. She was ready for some adventure. Besides, anything was better than the backseat of her car in a blizzard.

"Hang on there, I'm right here. My truck's right over there, can you make it?"

Julie eyed him suspiciously and he chuckled again.

"I promise I'm not some psychopath." He opened his hands wide in a, "who, me?" gesture. He couldn't hide the way the wrinkles around his eyes deepened at this exchange, but Julie was not amused.

"All psychopaths say they aren't psychopaths," Julie muttered. She quickly realized she didn't have a lot of options, though, and she was feeling a bit nauseous, colder by the second, and she was standing in her wet clothes in a blustery, snowy wind.

"Listen," he said, "You can't stay here. I'll get you somewhere safe and cozy and you can rest and we'll figure all this out in the morning. It's awfully late for you to be out here alone, even for Edgewood, and it's cold and supposed to be getting worse. The last time I saw it like this, we were socked in for at least a week. Let me get you fed and have Doc take a look at you in the morning. Do you have family you need to call?"

19

"Maybe I should give my car another try." She tried to smile but the worry creased her forehead.

"The house is just up the road, and it's warm and you can wait out the storm. At least come and eat dinner with us and we can go from there."

"No, I have my apple somewhere around here," She glanced around and spied her cheese sticks and a muck encrusted globe that resembled the once shiny apple she had paid thirteen cents for a moment ago. The stranger's gloved hand closed around it and he held it up like a prize trophy.

"Is this your dinner?" Snow landed on his eyelash and he blinked innocently. Julie's knees went even weaker.

She tried to be tough, frowning at first, but then she gave in and grinned with him.

"Yes, that's my dinner. It was either that or a slab of fast food, but they closed the gate on me before I could even get that." Wind pushed at her back, pushing her off balance and she was reminded of how cold it was.

"I'm Diego Garcia," the stranger put his hand out gallantly as Julie gazed up at him, squinting her own eyes in the haze and mist of snow. The parking lot was emptying around them, and the snow blasted silently through the haze of the lights glaring down on the area where they stood.

"Hi Diego," Julie murmured, forgetting her own name as she drowned in his blue eyes and dark eyelashes.

Diego grinned and grasped her hand.

"Do you have a name, or should I just call you

beautiful?"

Julie shook off the attraction, realizing she still hadn't introduced herself.

"Is that the line you use on every woman?" she smirked at his cheesy expression and disengaged her hand from Diego's. "I'm Julie Davenport, new resident of this local mud puddle." Her grin lit up the night and she matched his humor beat for beat.

Diego looked down at the apple and scrubbed it off on his coat. He handed her the freshly cleaned fruit and nodded at a large black truck an aisle over.

"That's my truck. Would you give me the pleasure of escorting you to the finest and *only* bed and breakfast in the area? Natalie will feed you and put you up for the night. In the morning you can figure out what you want to do with your car."

"You mean there aren't any hotels or anything?" Julie frantically scanned the horizon, but the dark night and glittering snow took away any visibility.

"Nope, welcome to Edgewood! No hotels, but like I said, the nicest bed and breakfast is just up the road. I'd be happy to take you."

Julie nodded in acquiescence, deciding to trust her intuition and not the newspaper hype about strange men in quiet parking lots.

"Let me just get some things." She nervously approached the door again. "I am pretty sure this door is what knocked me out a minute ago!" Inwardly she groaned at the sight of her keys still in the door. As quickly as she could, she leaned behind the seat and grabbed her overnight tote with the dog-eared novel her dad had given her just before he died. At the last second, she grabbed her mother's quilt, too.

Julie turned to catch Diego looking at her. She blushed and reached to lock the door, smacking her forehead on the glass of the window.

"Oh my gosh, I am just bound and determined to put myself in the hospital tonight!" She rubbed the knot that was forming on her head and Diego chuckled easily.

"Come on, let's get you home."

He grasped her elbow and took her tote from her. She gratefully allowed him to take charge as she put her keys in the pocket of her jacket and stepped toward his truck, tossing her purse straps over her shoulder. The truck fit him, but Julie had to use the helper bar to climb in. It was still warm from his drive over and she realized he hadn't done the shopping he had come to do.

"Don't you need to get something while you're here?" She looked at him, concerned she had interfered with his plans.

"Nah, nothing that I needed. I can always come back in the morning—if this snow lets up. I was just working on a project at Betty Lee's and needed some supplies. I think I might have the things I need in the garage already anyway." He grinned at her. "Not to worry, darlin'. I think you might be a more important project at the moment."

Chapter Five

Out of the corner of his eye, Diego watched as Julie leaned her head back. She looked exhausted, and he was pretty sure she'd given herself a concussion when she slipped by her car. He heard her soft sigh and a grin pulled at his lips. Some luck, to be thinking about being alone and all of a sudden he's got this gorgeous woman sitting next to him. He was grateful for the warm cab and soft country music that played quietly as he turned the diesel engine on. He wasn't really ready to unpack this and he wasn't sure what to say to her just yet, either. Within minutes they pulled into a long sloping driveway with a sign announcing Betty Lee's Bed and Breakfast. Diego had given Julie the grand tour of the small town, which amounted to two restaurants, three gas stations, a grocery store, a church and a library, besides the Wal-Mart, and all on the main strip that led to the Bed and Breakfast. Betty Lee's was a large two-story homestead with a rounded drive set back in the scrubby trees of the plains. Two wire reindeer pulled an old fashioned wagon decorated with Christmas lights on the lawn by the house.

Three gigantic dogs came barreling around the corner as Diego slipped the truck into park and shut off the engine. They leaped and barked at the truck, tails wagging, then as one, they turned and traipsed off around the house in the direction in which they had come.

"Your dogs?" Julie watched them wander off around the corner of the large adobe house that rose in the misty air, snow clinging to the eaves and filling in the corners of the window panes.

"A bunch of lovers. They talk a big game but they get distracted pretty fast. It's a good thing. Otherwise, you'd be flat on your back with three dogs licking your face in seconds." He hefted her tote and opened his door. "Here, I'll help you get down." He rounded the truck and was holding his hand out to help her out of the truck. Her hand was tiny and delicate in his, and the sleeve of her jacket coated his hand in muck, but he didn't mind. He was glad to have been there to rescue her, in fact. He could see she was pretty uncomfortable with being helped, and probably with being helpless. He would have felt the same way. He'd had a fair number of concussions in his day, though, and he knew that sometimes, just sitting quietly was all you could do. He figured she probably had a whopper of a headache, too.

"You okay?"

She nodded and hugged her purse to her chest as he

directed her toward the entrance. If he'd known her better, he might have laughed at the sight she made. She held her head high and fairly pranced through the snow that was already up to her knees. He heard her heave a deep breath and realized she was probably terrified. Alone? Stuck? Natalie would know what to do to set her mind at ease. All he knew was that he was suddenly pretty hungry himself.

Diego stomped his feet as he opened the door to the front entrance, kicking the snow off the treads of his workboots and effectively announcing his presence. He felt, rather than saw her look up at him with a question on her face.

"Don't worry about your wet shoes. Just come warm up by the fire, and I'll get a room set up for you so you can get more comfortable. We can throw those in the washer in a minute."

He set Julie's tote on the floor and held the door open, gesturing for her to enter first. She thanked him quietly and looked around as he removed his jacket and hung it on the old tack hook Natalie had repurposed as a hat rack. She'd used the center of a split log that lay flat against the paneling that lined the room. It already housed a cowboy hat and a third empty hook, where he put Julie's coat when she pulled it off.

"I'll get you a towel and then I'll see where Natalie is and if there is anything to eat." He stepped to the door of the kitchen and turned back to look at his stray. Diego's gaze slid over the jeans that molded her slim form, and which, by now, had to be very uncomfortable.

The slush had soaked that smooth round derriere and the hem of her sweater was coated with mud. She was beautiful, no doubt about that. Her long wavy blonde hair had smelled heavenly as he had leaned over her in the parking lot. He had been so concerned about her when he saw her on the ground, he could have kissed her when she woke up. Her prickly retort pushed that idea out of his mind, but only for a moment, and his reactions to each moment had been a surprise to him. She had the most enticing eyes he had ever looked into, changing colors like the tide as waves crashed over the beach. He would bet she was as tumultuous as the ocean too, or at least as the December weather on the prairies of New Mexico. Maybe it had just been her concussion messing with her pupils. Either way, he was intrigued.

He was sizing her up, trying to figure out what a beautiful woman was doing in a strange town alone in a snowstorm, and at Christmas, but without family to visit. He understood that cars broke down, but how many women just walked into his life like that? Especially when he had just been pondering the notion of love and his keen desire for it minutes before. It was irrational, but he found himself wondering about this woman. He didn't really believe in random coincidence, and the idea of fate or chance was foreign as well, but she seemed different from the women who threw themselves at him, hoping to ride on his reputation and his pursestrings. She was quiet, reserved, and he could sense an infinite sadness surrounding her. She definitely was not like most women who followed the rodeo circuit. Maybe he was just hoping she was different. Maybe, he hoped, the universe had tossed up a chance.

She turned to catch him watching her and he slipped out of the room to grab a towel and find Natalie. Time for some food.

Chapter Six

A blazing fire welcomed her as she put out her hands to warm them. The room was cavernous, yet cozy, and she immediately felt enveloped by warmth and an overwhelming fatigue, even though her hands were so cold the heat gave them the sudden needles and tingles of blood finally moving. This was a room to relax in. She could fall asleep if she sat down, wet jeans and all. Everywhere she turned, there was texture. Jute runners on the buffet and along the stone bench in front of the fireplace. Cowhide on the floor. Sheepskin on the sofa. Wooden vigas overhead and exposed adobe bricks added to the rustic ambience, their old world charm adding to the aged, yet elegant appearance of the home. *Good thing I'm not a vegetarian*, she thought. Diego returned with a towel and his hand brushed against hers as he handed it over. She trembled with what felt like a spark. *Get it together, sister.*

Gratefully, Julie wrapped the towel around her shoulders. Diego was hospitable and she appreciated it, but she figured her clothes would dry soon and she'd have to ask for a ride back to her car. She was frustrated. The place was beautiful, and he seemed very nice, but Julie hated losing a single stitch of her independence. After she'd left Adam, she'd fought long and hard to figure who that independent woman was. This woman right now didn't feel like herself. Something for her headache, dry clothes, and then she needed to hit the road.

"Let me just go find out about some food, then," Diego left the room again, leaving Julie to acquaint herself with the landscape of the Bed and Breakfast. She stood and turned her backside to the flame, hoping to dry her jeans before Diego came back into the room. Food really did sound pretty good, after all.

The casual elegance Julie had noticed moments before echoed the western lifestyle and its sentiments through a variety of paintings, photos and sketches. She was especially drawn to a pencil sketch of a rope draped over a saddle horn, a gloved hand resting on top of both. It was simple, and gorgeous. It captured the confident swagger of the cowboy icon. She turned her body to face the fire and noticed the framed photographs on the mantel, half expecting a framed photograph of John Wayne to jump out at her. A young couple and several of Diego with children smiled out at

Julie and she noticed others of an older couple. *Probably his parents*, she thought, and smiled at the photo of Diego sitting astride a beautiful horse.

I wonder who these other people are, and if these are Diego's kids. Julie blinked and shook her head when she recognized the subtle jealousy that was creeping over her, seeing this happy family. Realizing she was mostly jealous of a supposed wife of a man she had just met, she shrugged and tried to eliminate the feelings that she couldn't explain. Maybe it was just that she had never been able to fulfill that picture in her life, try as she might. A year before, she had thought she had the chance for that, but things change, and sometimes they change fast. She heard Diego come back once again and she turned to face him. Her hands were finally almost warm, and she was more relaxed.

"I brought you some tea," he said, as he crossed the room to stand next to the fireplace. I added a touch of honey. I hope you like it that way. Something tells me you have a sweet tooth." He grinned as he handed the drink over.

"I do, thank you so much." Julie accepted the mug and her newly warmed hands seemed to burn against the sides, the aftermath of having been so cold. She breathed in the steam and smiled up at him, grateful once again for his thoughtfulness. "I feel so much better already, thank you for taking me in." She took a sip of the steaming liquid and sighed. "This is perfect," she smiled, but her expression quickly faded to concern. "I don't want to be a burden, so maybe you can take me back to my car and I'll be on my way?"

Diego nodded but said grimly, "I don't know if that will be as easy as all that sounds. Natalie just told me that they were shutting down the freeway. The canyon can be deadly under the right conditions. If your car won't start and needs work, that will take a day or two. Especially with it being so close to Christmas. Most people have closed down around here."

Julie looked into her mug as if she could read the patterns in the steam. "I was afraid you'd say that." She looked up. "And there are no hotels?"

"You're standing in what amounts to the front lobby of the only place around. You are welcome to stay as long as you need. Anyway, Natalie's been itching for some company lately, since her friend Kristy moved into town. She's in the kitchen getting some dinner ready for you."

"I don't know how much company I'd be." Julie realized how pathetic she sounded and squared her shoulders. "I guess I didn't really have to be in a hurry anyway."

"Oh, I'm sure once you get warmed up, fed, and have a hot shower, you'll be a whole new woman." He gestured at her pants, and she looked down, chagrined. "Would you like to change, and then get something to eat?"

"I think I'm about dried out, except my sneakers." She made a squishing sound with her toes as they moved in the shoes. "But I'd love something to eat. I think that apple got a little bruised when it hit the ground."

Julie watched him arrange his face into a warm smile

as he thought about how to ask her "How're you holding up?" She knew her face was pale because she could see her reflection in the mirror behind his head. Her eyeballs ached to try and sort the details in the room. "How's your head?" he continued, teasing, "I imagine *it* got a little bruised when it hit the ground."

"Oh, I think I'm okay; a little queasy, but I'll live. This tea hit the spot." Julie winced and put her hand out to the mantel to balance herself as a wave of dizziness rippled through her. "But maybe I should sit down a spell." She missed the spark of concern that lashed through Diego's bright blue irises, but she felt his hand steady her.

"Of course, here, let's get you into the kitchen. That's always the best place in the house." He led her toward a voice that was singing some Christmas song that Julie decided was original. It definitely didn't ring familiar to her ears. But then, she hadn't listened to Christmas music in a few years herself anyway. She no longer desired the half-hearted joy it seemed to bring most people. She downright detested it, in fact.

The kitchen was an explosion of light, warmth and sound. Natalie was an energetic redhead who seemed to buzz around the kitchen. Julie immediately smelled stew in the air and her stomach grumbled, even though her brain told her it wasn't sure it was a good idea to eat after the knock her head had taken. Julie never was one to listen to her brain when her stomach was involved. The sight of Natalie scooping out thick chunks of beef and slices of carrots and onions made her mouth water. How long had it been since Julie had eaten a hot meal prepared by someone skilled in the kitchen? Julie no longer even ate out at restaurants, preferring sandwiches and bowls of cereal to spending the time or money to cook. A gourmet meal in Julie's kitchen might consist of macaroni and cheese out of the box.

"Sweetheart! How are you feeling?" Natalie bustled over and took Julie by the arm and led her over to the table. Diego politely made the introductions and sat across from Julie after pulling out a chair for her to rest.

"Natalie makes the best beef stew you've ever tasted," Diego grinned up at the buxom redhead. Julie bit her lip watching the exchange, feeling that sudden unfamiliar twinge of jealousy at the comfort the two obviously displayed. "I told Natalie that you fell in the parking lot at the store and knocked your head a good one. Do you think you can eat?"

"I can eat. I'm okay. I have a headache, but I'll live." Julie smiled at his concern and pulled her chair closer to the table.

"Let me take a look at you." Natalie stepped closer, and Julie saw the concern etch a wrinkle between her brows.

"I think I'm okay, really." Julie took a deep breath. "Wow. It smells wonderful in here." Julie cleared her throat shyly and asked, "How far am I from a city?"

Natalie placed a bowl of beef stew and some warmed tortillas in front of Julie. "Darlin', you are about a world away from a city, although Albuquerque really isn't very far. In this weather, though, it might as well be across the ocean."

Julie was distracted by Diego's long fingers as he reached for a tortilla and added some salt to his stew. His nails were closely cropped and tidy. She bit her lip and looked down into her lap.

"It's 30 minutes on a good day through the canyon," he said and took a bite of beef.

Natalie nodded. "But with this snow and wind, and especially with the temperature dropping so quickly, you'd be lucky to even make it in two hours. Besides, Jessica over at the office said the freeway was already shutting down, and even in the truck, it would be slow. It's treacherous at times, and tonight it is going to be at its worst. I heard the weatherman say to buckle in; it's going to be a good one. The last time we had a major storm, we were snowed in for two weeks! They had to airdrop feed for stranded stock. Poor Diego lost a third of his heifers and the pigs took a beating too. Lucky for him, Governor Slack declared a state of emergency and he was able to get some help. Since then, he's built up some shelters for the stock in case it ever happened again." Natalie finally took a breath and sat across from Julie, obviously grateful for the company. "I'm sorry to talk your ear off here when you're so tired. My kids are asleep and it's been ages since someone my age has spent any time at Betty Lee's! The Bed and Breakfast industry isn't exactly booming, especially because it's so darn close to Albuquerque and cheaper, more accessible hotels and amenities."

Julie smiled and took a bite, content to listen to Natalie patter on. She slyly watched Diego nod in agreement and then stand to refill his bowl. She chewed on the tender beef and tore off a chunk of tortilla.

"That was a rough winter. It would stop snowing for a day, start to melt, and then it would snow again. It caked the snow down for several feet. Couldn't shovel it, cattle couldn't move, the tractors didn't even do much." Diego returned to the table.

"Then it finally melted and we had to deal with the mud!" Natalie shook her head at the memory. "The trucks could barely get in and out with that mud."

"So, this is a ranch too?" Julie couldn't help the interested tone that invaded her voice as she asked the question.

"That's an understatement!" Natalie proudly smiled, and nodded at Diego. "He owns a thousand acres."

Diego quietly blushed, a characteristic that endeared him to Julie even more as she gazed at him over her dinner. She couldn't imagine being rescued by a more handsome cowboy than the one who sat across from her at the moment. She could imagine those strong fingers stroking the skin along her spine. She shivered at that thought and quickly looked down at her dinner again. How callous she felt, especially when the woman she assumed was his wife sat next to her!

Natalie eyed her suspiciously.

"Let me see your eyes." Julie thought for a minute that Natalie was going to accuse her of the sentiments she just admitted into her head, but as she watched Natalie grab a flashlight and move to her side, she realized Natalie was concerned that Julie might have a concussion. The wrinkle between her brows had returned.

"Do you feel nauseous or dizzy?" Natalie flashed the light in Julie's eye and made Julie follow her finger from side to side. Julie's brain knocked into the side of her skull each time her eyes pulled to the side with Natalie's finger.

"I did, but I feel a lot better now." Julie lied shamelessly and her head ached in rhythm to her heartbeat. The concern and comfort displayed toward her by complete strangers was overwhelming. "That stew was incredible and did me a world of good. I don't think I hit that hard anyway." Julie pushed her hair back from her face and took another sip of the tea that had gone tepid as she had shoveled the stew down.

Diego snorted. "You hit hard enough to knock yourself out! How much harder do you think you could have taken? Natalie, remember when we were little and you did the same thing on the pond out back?" He turned his eyes on Julie, "She didn't wake up for half an hour! Mom and dad were so worried she'd knocked out a chunk of her brain that they damn near killed themselves getting her off the ice and into the house!"

Julie looked from Diego to the woman standing above her. "So you knew each other as kids too?"

It was Natalie's turn to snort, waving an impatient hand in Diego's direction. "That jackass is my brother!" She moved to the counter and replaced the flashlight in a drawer under the microwave. "He was the one who knocked me over on that pond! He makes it sound so innocent, but he was in such a hurry to skate to the other side that he pushed past me and I wiped out."

Julie couldn't help the relief that flooded through her at that statement. She looked at her bowl of stew, pulled her chair back in, and speared a carrot. A smile tweaked the corners of her mouth as she listened to the two exchange banter about childhood experiences. For some reason, she was enormously grateful that the man who rescued her was not married to this gorgeous bundle of energy. She just hoped there wasn't another woman floating around here somewhere. She hadn't noticed any in the pictures, but whose kids were in the pictures with Diego? This was a mystery she might be inclined to solve, if she weren't so tired and if she could just think straight.

"Well, you must be tired after your adventure tonight," Julie thought he must be reading her mind. She looked slowly up at him and slid her spoon into the bowl.

"Exhausted." She languidly watched as he took her dishes to the sink. Her hand dropped limply from the table to her lap and she reached for her glass.

"If you have a concussion, it looks mild, but I can see you have a whopper of a headache. You probably can go to bed." Natalie bustled about the kitchen, putting dishes in the sink and wiping the crumbs from the table. "I'll show you to a room and a bathroom so you can freshen up and hit the hay."

Julie looked gratefully over her shoulder at Diego and called, "Thank you for rescuing me." She smiled and he tipped an imaginary hat after her as she was bundled out of the kitchen.

Chapter Seven

After finishing the tidying in the kitchen, Diego closed the kitchen door quietly behind him and headed out to his small casita. He had surprised himself with his offer. He had just considered the damage strange women had done to him in his life, and here he was, offering a complete stranger a place to stay where his sister could do a number. And then he had fed her in their mother's kitchen! He felt himself go tender when he had watched her eyes drop with fatigue. He shook his head as he pounded the snow off his boots on the front porch. He was a little concerned about the concussion, but Natalie didn't seem too worried. He trusted Natalie when it came to that. He was proud of his sister and knew she knew what she was doing. He whistled once and the dogs materialized next to him, pushing past him into his living room, trailing snow and ice as they went.

She was gorgeous. He was smitten and he didn't even know her beyond her name.

He grabbed the dust broom and followed behind the boys, sweeping up as he moved into the house, his thoughts on the long golden ringlets of hair he'd had to untangle from his gloves.

Cooper jumped onto the ottoman and started gnawing on an antler they had found in the woods before the storm. The other two snuffled in their food, and noisily drank water. Undeterred, Diego's thoughts followed their course. Natalie was the true test. She was easy to get along with on the surface, but she was also an excellent judge of character. If Patti was any witness, cross Natalie once, and you would be dog food, get her to love you, and she was forever after trying to make you his wife. Needless to say, Patti was hamburger meat in Natalie's eyes. The freeway incident had been the last straw, but to hear Natalie tell it, she'd lost any respect for Patti as a human the day she overheard Patti telling someone on the phone how easy it was going to be to live a life of luxury at Diego's expense. Diego had no idea about Julie, but when he watched her blue eyes fill with tears in the parking lot of the store, his heart seemed to melt a little in his chest.

He shouldn't have taken her home. She was going to cause him trouble, but somehow, he expected it was different from Patti trouble. He could feel it in his bones. Julie was as different from Patti as Cooper was from the other dogs. He laughed at the way Natalie had bustled about, sizing Julie up, and he knew he was going to get an earful in the morning. Not only was Julie gorgeous, but she was independent and strong. Diego lit a fire, poured a drink, and settled in for the evening, imagining how nice it was going to be to see her in the morning.

Chapter Eight

The room was warm and cozy, just like the rest of the house, and was clearly designed as an oasis of peace and serenity. The accents of deep red and shades of dark browns soothed her senses as she glanced at the down covered bed. More texture of brushed sheepskin covered the floor beneath her feet and she could easily have sunk to the floor and slept peacefully there. Sleep beckoned, but she headed for the bathroom first. She felt like a character in a fairy tale, only this one could very easily have a bad ending. But wow, what a gorgeous house. *Good place to die*, she thought, cynically.

The personal powder room was just as nice as if she had stepped into the Ritz. Dark brown tile covered the floors and walls and the claw-footed tub invited with its Siren's call. *I could easily get used to this*, Julie thought. She was tempted to run a bath, but a yawn overtook her desire for pampering. Not only was sleep beckoning, but now it was a frantic reminder of the type of day she'd had. If she was honest, she was tired from the type of year she'd had. From the other room, her cell phone buzzed a reminder that a message awaited.

"Julie? Hi, honey, it's me, Adam. Baby, I wish you'd answer." She heard him sigh heavily and she cringed momentarily. "I miss you so much." His false tone reminded her of the car salesman who assured her the Sebring was a good buy. It had been a good buy–most of the time. Adam wished her a happy Christmas before he clicked off. She sighed in disgust and hit delete on the voicemail. She couldn't understand why he felt the need to call and harass her just because it was Christmas. Was it a misguided sense of still loving her, or was it a lasting guilt over what he had done to her with her best friend? Honestly, she couldn't decide what she was more upset about. Losing him, or losing Sara. The more she thought about it, the more she knew it had always been the pain of being replaced. It wasn't so much that they were together. If Sara chose

Adam, after all of the late night conversations she'd had with her about him, then she could have him. But being replaced...that cut deeper than she cared to admit.

When Julie had walked into the overpriced apartment she shared with Adam twelve months ago, she hadn't been too shocked to realize that he was not alone. She had walked in on him two times before with women he worked with. Each time, she had overlooked it and moved on, forgiving him and taking him back. Each time had gotten harder. The hurt the first time was like bad poetry and she cried herself to sleep more often than she admitted, but she felt like she somehow had deserved it. She told herself that maybe she could have done more to keep him inspired. The second time, she cried a little less, but she had also been really distracted at work, and she knew that she was leaving him out of her attention span. That third time, though, had made her furious. He was with her best friend. She wondered about that now. He had sugar coated his reasons, telling her he'd change, that he loved her, that it was a mistake. Twice. Three times. Maybe more that she was unaware of. Julie wasn't entirely sure. And she still wondered why she hadn't realized he could never change. The last time had been the hardest, but the easiest to set her straight. She knew it was over that night. Two days later she'd returned to Amarillo and filed for divorce.

She couldn't remember what she did in those two days, but she knew it had involved that stashed bottle of wine and several others in a hotel with a pretty comfortable bed. She hadn't spoken to Sara since, though Sara had tried to call several times. Adam, on the other hand, she had spoken to several times, though not because she had wanted to. He would call her at work. He left messages daily on her cell phone. She finally changed her email address because he had sent so many sickening pictures of flowers...and other things. He had begged her and pleaded with her to come back to him, to move home, to share his life, he was a changed man, he made a mistake, all of the lines she had listened to him make so many times before. This time, she knew he would never change, and since that Christmas, she had decided she would take a trip every few months. She had gone north, south, east, and to celebrate this first Christmas completely alone, she was going west. She had planned to get to Sedona, Arizona, but she hadn't gotten very far before, like clockwork, Adam was calling her, asking her to come home. She sighed and hit the delete button after each message. She could never take him back. She never knew she was stubborn, but Adam was really helping her see personality characteristics she had never really thought about. Stubborn was just one of them. Obstinate was beginning to become another. If he called her one more time, she was likely to throw the phone out the window of her Chrysler...if she ever got it to run again.

It wounded her pride every time he called, but it had devastated her to finally realize he was not the man she thought she had married. His indiscretions were heartbreaking at first, but when she found him with Sara, her heart cracked in two and filled with concrete.

The icing on the cake was that he wrecked her most favorite holiday and ruined her surprise visit. She finally changed. She closed up inside, erecting walls that hadn't been torn down by a single person since. Three years before, when her parents had died, she had looked to Adam for support and he had failed miserably. She had sunk her grief into a relationship she knew didn't have the depth to survive, and yet, it had lasted for a few years. Sara had failed her too, and she didn't ever want to hurt like that again, so it was safer to close herself off to the world. Maybe she had even closed herself off to herself.

No matter, she sighed. *I'm happy alone anyway. I don't want Adam and I don't need anyone. But I sure wouldn't mind having a handsome cowboy like Diego to warm me up on nights like this.* Still, Adam's call had tightened her shoulders and frazzled her brain. When would he get the message? She dropped her earrings onto the bureau and tilted her head to look at her reflection in the mirror.

"He'll keep calling because he's selfish and self-absorbed," she mumbled as she slipped her stiff, but dry jeans off over her feet. She was looking forward to a shower, because she was having a hard time putting her mind to rest. She tossed her sweater in the growing pile of dirty clothes by the bedroom door and stood for a minute in her underwear.

The bed was tempting, but she felt weary and wrung out. She remembered the way Diego had found her in the puddle and an image of his blue eyes seared her brain. She shook herself and wrapped her arms in a comforting hug. He might be beautiful, but this was all too convenient and she wasn't used to having things come easy. Sedona was still calling her name, after all.

After a quick shower, Julie was ready for bed. She braided her hair rather than drying it and slung it over her shoulder. The king sized bed was covered in the thickest down blanket Julie had ever felt. The sheets were a crisp snowy white, adorned with simple red embroidery. She decided she suddenly knew what Heaven felt like as she slid between them, sinking into the downy softness of the pillows, the cushioned top of the mattress cradling her hips. Feeling the exhaustion take over, and ignoring the throbbing in her head, the dampness sinking into her pillow from her still wet hair, and the irritation of being thwarted in her travel plans, Julie closed her eyes and promptly fell asleep, her last image one of a tall, dark, handsome cowboy gently holding her head in his hands.

Chapter Nine

Julie woke to a crisp morning and a banging headache. She reached up and felt the knot under her hair and winced as the nerves screamed. She sighed and stretched, vaguely remembering how she had gotten into the heavenly bed she found herself in now.

She flipped the covers off and smirked at her dumb luck.

Some way to meet a man, she thought, and rolled out of bed, groaning the whole time. She hadn't had a concussion since she was a kid and Tony Morris pushed her off the top of the aluminum slide. She stood slowly and moved to the window, pushing back the quilted curtains that hid the view of the deepening snow that still fell outside the house. Julie noticed the thick clouds that still threatened days of snow that would add to the blanket on the ground. It appeared that several inches, maybe even feet had fallen in the night. Concerned she wouldn't be able to leave, even if she could get her car fixed, Julie grabbed some warm fuzzy socks out of her bag and the robe that Natalie had lent her and rushed downstairs. The house was silent. It appeared that either no one was awake or no one was around.

When she got to the kitchen, she smelled hot coffee and realized she was not alone after all. Diego sat at the table quietly reading the newspaper. He smiled at her as she took him in, his long legs encased in dark denim jeans, a red and black checked shirt buttoned snugly over long john underwear that peeked out from the top button that was not fastened.

Julie's hand flew to her head again, realizing she hadn't even looked in the mirror this morning in her haste to get downstairs. She had gone to bed with her hair still wet last night, and it was probably standing in twenty different directions because she knew the braid had come loose. As it was, she was right. She ran her hands through her hair nervously, desperately trying to tame the stray hairs without giving her nerves away.

"Mornin' ma'am," he drawled, lifting his coffee mug to her in greeting. "Would you like some coffee?"

"You read my mind." Her face lit up and quickly darkened as she thought, *oh, forget it. I'm leaving in a few minutes anyway. I'll never see this gorgeous man again.* Sadness streaked through her at that, along with surprise and shock that she might be feeling this after having just met him. She moved toward the table as Diego rose to pour her a cup.

She caught his glance as she sat in a chair next to the one he had just vacated and her face colored again. He pulled a ceramic mug out of the cupboard and filled it with steaming coffee. "How did you sleep?" He asked as he set the mug in front of Julie. She wrapped both hands around it and smiled at him.

"I slept like a rock. That bed was perfect."

"How is your head today? Feeling better?" He pushed the sugar and cream closer to her and watched her turn her coffee sweet with the sugar.

"Oh, I feel better. You have all been so nice, and I really appreciate your hospitality." She didn't lie often, but she also was not going to be a pansy about a headache in front of this guy. She sipped the coffee and grinned appreciatively. "You sure know how to make a good cup of coffee!" She hesitated after she said that. That had always been on the top of her "man list," though Adam had never fit the bill. He couldn't make a good cup of coffee to save his life. If Julie had a dollar for every time she cringed at a sip, she would be a rich woman.

"Such a simple thing." She mused aloud.

"What's that?"

"Making a good cup of coffee seems so simple, and yet," she peered at him over the rim of the mug, "so many are incapable of pulling it off."

Diego watched her intently. "I didn't think making coffee was so hard."

"Oh, you'd be surprised." Julie's eyes flickered at the irony of the difference between what she knew about Adam and what she was realizing she wanted to know about this man.

"About what I owe—" Julie's voice caught as she noticed his dark blue eyes boring into her own. The smile that flirted with his lips made her shiver. Those lips were magnets for her eyes. She licked her own nervously and stumbled over the words. "Um, I didn't see a bill for my stay here last night."

"Don't worry about payment right now." His deep voice rumbled over her and she felt like she practically swayed into him. *You're such an idiot, but wow, that voice.* She could hardly hear him over her own thoughts. "We don't know how long it will be before your car is ready, and really, with this snow, you might be here awhile." The look on his face made Julie wonder if that was such a bad thing. She wrestled with that for a minute, feelings starting to bounce around in the cage of her head.

"Really, I couldn't." She fidgeted with the handle of the coffee mug and glanced around the room, anywhere but at the man who had so completely captured her attention in the span of about eight hours. Six of which she had been asleep for. "I'd like to make arrangements, if I can."

"Let's worry about it later," Diego insisted. "It's Christmas, there's a hell of a snowstorm out there, and it's warm in here. We've got all the time in the world to do business."

"You can't make money like that."

"I think about more important things than money."

She rose to stand near the window. The kitchen had large windows that rose almost from the floor to the ceiling. Already the snow covered the lower sill of the window where Julie stood. Thoughts of being stranded and alone fled as she gazed at the glistening backdrop that shimmered in and out of the fog on the other side of the window pane. It was incredible, really. The mountains flirted with her eyes, glittering from behind the snowflakes that danced before her. The land spread far and wide, and she sighed gently, falling deeply in love with what she knew didn't belong to her.

It's still snowing outside." She murmured over her cup. "I can't quite believe it!" Julie could feel herself chattering nervously and had a hard time stopping. Diego had the most piercing eyes she had ever looked into, and she had dealt with a lot of people in her time. She was grateful to be looking out the window at the moment. She felt out of her element.

"Yeah, it doesn't usually get this bad. We're supposedly looking at a few days more of this." He picked up his own cup of coffee and gazed lazily at Julie unabashedly. "Do you get much snow where you're

48

from?" He paused and looked at her quizzically. "Where are you from?"

"Amarillo," she sighed, without taking her eyes from the landscape out the window.

***

Diego stood and leaned at the sink, his long legs crossed at the ankle. The woman before him was adorable. Sure, her hair was sticking out in a couple of directions, but it added to what he was beginning to think was her sweet nature. The robe Natalie had leant her wasn't the sexiest of creations, but it sure offered things for him to think about, and his imagination was active enough to make him think those things as he watched her look out the window. He turned and topped off his mug of coffee.

"Amarillo, huh? I've done some business over there." He thought about her admission. Geography wasn't a tell tale sign, but he was really hoping she was as innocent as she looked. Truth was, he had won several steer wrestling competitions in Amarillo, including a world title that had been his last. That was where the magazine, *Cowboy Historian*, had made him a cover feature, and that was where he'd met Patti, who had followed him here and still occasionally made his life a living hell.

Julie turned back to him and blinked. "Really? What business is that?"

He didn't want to answer the question. He had been hoping the conversation would not turn to rodeos and his successes. He could not deal with another Patti in his life. Had Julie found him and followed him here too?

He grew nervous at the thought, wishing his success had not been so successful. It had thrown too many gold diggers his way, and the rodeo was long in his past. Too many women had appeared on his doorstep or here at the Bed and Breakfast looking for what he might offer because they thought he was a hero or a cowboy. After he'd been featured in the magazine, his phone had blown up and Natalie teased him that he was never going to get a moment's peace. His paranoia irritated him, so he worked to channel that energy into something else.

He was content with his quiet life and his small ranch in the middle of nowhere. The magazine had been a mistake, and he'd thought the hype had died down, but he wondered if this woman was yet another one of the same. He wanted a woman who would love him for his other features, rather than for some high-blown notoriety created by the media. *Don't be so stupid,* he thought. *She's just shown up, and you know nothing about her, much less whether you can love her. Or whether she might fall in love with you.* He thought of how to answer her question without giving too much information.

"I recently sold some cattle that way."

"Oh," Julie said.

He hoped she was as clueless to the cattle industry and to him as she appeared to be. He could see she struggled with whether to ask more questions, and he watched her decide to sip her coffee instead. *That's a good sign.* He was glad to see that she appeared to be intelligent and discerning. At least she didn't pretend to

50

know something she didn't. Or so he assumed. He hoped he was right.

Abruptly Diego turned and dumped his coffee in the sink. "Natalie and the kids are out with Gabe looking for a Christmas tree. Would you like to go follow them or would you like to stay here? They just left about ten minutes ago." He turned back to look at Julie. "Of course, if you want, you can come with me to check on the cattle. I've got to take the snowmobile out to the shelter to see if they used the brains God graced them with to get in out of this snow."

"Oh gosh, that's right! Christmas is in just a few days!"

Of all the things to unpack, she selected the idea that Christmas was a couple of days away. Diego wondered how she could have forgotten. He cocked his head and wished he hadn't dumped his coffee. A good slug of java would have been welcomed. It would at least mask the smile he felt tugging at his cheeks.

"Uh, maybe I should go try to get my car running and get on the road." Diego watched her dip her head back to her coffee, and wondered if she had any idea how cute she was. She wasn't going anywhere in this weather, dead car or not. She wasn't going to get a mile down the road before she would have to turn back. He weighed how much he told her. Natalie was a fireball when he tried to explain some things to her. She called it "mansplaining" and she wanted nothing to do with it. Granted, Natalie was pretty smart, and she could fix a tractor as easily as Frank could usually, she just preferred to cook and play with the kids. Diego knew he had a tendency to repeat himself and several girlfriends had accused him of being condescending, even though he thought he was just helpful. He decided to tread delicately with this woman. He didn't know how she felt about hearing some things from a man, much less from him, and he was working at being better.

"I've already called Joe over at the service station, and he said there's no way anything is going to get done today on anybody's car. He's snowed in at his place, and there isn't much hope of a let-up in the weather." *There. That was straightforward and to the point.* Diego leaned easily against the counter, his arms crossed, he knew he probably looked aggressive, so he calmed the muscles by his mouth. Patti used to tell him he looked angry and suspicious when he was tense like this. He remained watchful, waiting to see which emotion would settle on her face. Right now she was clearly going through several of them. Her eyebrows had hit her hairline at first, and then her face reddened, and now she was looking down at the coffee cup that she had already drained.

"Oh."

"Yeah. It looks like you're stuck."

Julie played with the edge of the tablecloth. "Well, shoot. What am I going to do?"

Diego wondered if she was asking him or talking to herself. She seemed to hold a lot of conversations with herself, not really inviting anyone in. He couldn't figure out why that bothered him so much.

"If you ask me," he started, "I'd call your friends or

family and let them know you won't be able to make it for a few days."

"I don't have any family." She spoke matter of factly and Diego's eyes softened slightly.

"Well, I think this storm has settled in for a bit, and you won't be able to get on the freeway anyway." Julie opened her mouth to speak, but Diego continued his end of the conversation, even though part of him was a little nervous she'd snap at him. He could see her frustration build with every word he spoke. "Your car isn't reliable right now anyway. Just stay with us for awhile. I promise, we don't bite." He grinned at this and hoped she realized he was right. On the other hand, Patti wasn't so far out of his memory. Diego almost kicked himself at how easy he was making this for her.

Dammit, what if she was a gold digger? He worried she might be like the last crazy woman to stalk him. He'd almost been thrown in jail himself, trying to get Patti out of his life. But how could Julie have known he'd be at the store at the exact moment that she was walking out? *You're going crazy old fella. She has no idea who you are.* He talked himself out of the thought as quickly as it came. He watched her pull her hair back and stretch like the tomcat that lived in the back of Ginger's stall. She visibly relaxed in front of his eyes. He realized she had made a decision in her mind without speaking a word. He kind of liked that she had conversations with herself. It clearly helped her work through her thoughts.

"Actually, I don't have anyone to see anyway. I

wasn't going to visit friends, I..." Her voice trailed off and she stood quickly. "I don't have any clothes that I can wear out in this weather, so I guess I'll have to stay inside."

"Nonsense," Diego pushed off the counter and moved toward the door. "Natalie left some stuff for you." Julie hesitated and then followed Diego.

"I'd like it if you went with me, Julie,"

"Where are we going?"

Chapter Ten

Within minutes, Julie was dressed in the long silk underwear, the long sleeved undershirt and the hand-knitted woolen sweater that fit like it had been made for her. She climbed into the black and gray quilted overalls and snapped the buttons into the boots that also fit just right. She didn't really think she'd need all of this gear, but Diego hadn't stopped handing her items of clothing and he told her to put all of it on or she'd regret it. His last words as he'd walked out, leaving her to change, were along the lines of wanting to make sure she didn't freeze her butt off out there, as he happened to like it the way it was. Julie had blushed furiously and quickly closed the door behind him.

She headed toward the door and heard Diego coming to meet her. He had on a heavy brown down jacket with black canvas overalls and was carrying thick gloves and a slab of ham in a biscuit.

"Here, I forgot you didn't eat anything earlier. This is something to tide you over for awhile." He grinned a little out of the side of his mouth. "I guess I'm rushing you a bit, huh?"

Julie nodded but quickly said, "It's okay; I'm looking forward to meeting your cows." She could have hit herself on the forehead at that statement, but her arm wouldn't move in the shoulder.

Diego laughed. "You look a little padded there. You doin' okay?"

Julie laughed too. "I'm definitely feeling like that little boy in "A Christmas Story" right now. If I fall over, you'll have to help me up!" She waddled around in a circle like a sumo wrestler, grinning at the chuckles this elicited from Diego. Already, she loved the sound of his laugh, and his easy smile drew her eyes. She lingered on his lips, unconsciously licking her own. He had the most intriguing pair. She could imagine him kissing her in so many places, and right now, those places were making her even warmer in the snowsuit. Her eyes widened as his grin grew even larger.

"So," she said quickly, "shall we?"

Diego gallantly opened the door and held it as Julie stepped outside. Immediately she realized how grateful she was for the extra padding. Briskly cold, the wind blustered gigantic snowflakes in her face and eyes. She turned her head to cut the wind and Diego stepped into her view.

"This way, the snowmobile is in the barn over here." His long legs ate up the distance quickly, and Julie had to run to keep up, which was no easy feat in the snow clothes she had on at the moment.

The barn was large enough to accommodate a camper and several four-wheelers and still have a large enough space for storage and to house several animals. Julie could smell the aromatic alfalfa hay in the back and heard the horses snorting and clomping in their stalls. She wandered over to find a small paint horse poking her head over the door of the stall curiously.

"That's Ginger," Diego said, coming around behind Julie, giving her senses a jolt as she smelled his own scent of ginger and lemon mixed with the earthy smell of the farm. She realized he was awakening something in her and it surprised and excited her, while at the same time, made her feel timid and uncertain.

Diego lightly placed his hand on Julie's back and nudged her closer to the stall.

"Go on, touch her. She's gentle and she loves to have her chin rubbed." He showed Julie how to scratch Ginger just right and Julie giggled when the warm snout of the beautiful horse nuzzled into her elbow.

"She's so soft," Julie breathed. Her wonder was evident at the gentle nature of such a large creature. When Julie was little, she'd seen horses at the petting zoo, but she had always been afraid of their hooves and teeth. Not Ginger, though. Julie was in love with the big doe eyes and the way she seemed to have bangs hanging down her forehead.

"Yeah, she's a softie alright. And she acts like it too. She'd nurse a wolf if it would let her. She doesn't have the sense in her head to run when she's supposed to, nor the care to." Fondly, he scrubbed the side of Ginger's neck with his fingers and patted her on the shoulder.

"Why did you name her Ginger, when she has these splotches of color?" Julie continued to rub Ginger's chin and nose and rested her forehead against the dun colored snout.

***

Silently, Diego watched Julie begin to breathe in his life. He sensed that this woman was hurting from something and it made him want to wrap his arms around her and protect her from the world. He had never felt this way for a woman and was startled at the depth of his reaction. The thoughts of her being a gold-digging rodeo hound were fading as he watched her innocently fall in love with his horse. She hadn't displayed a single iota of recognition, and besides, it had been awhile since he'd been in Amarillo anyway. She was a far cry from the aggressive and fiesty Patti, but he had a feeling Julie was just as powerful in personality, given time.

He shook his head and turned away from the stall. He busied himself with getting feed for the horses.

"My mother named her Ginger for her favorite character in a book." His memories floated over his shoulder as he poured grain in the feed bucket and checked the water level in Ginger's trough. "Mom never really cared much for the way something looked on the outside, she cared about the feelings those things inspired on the inside." Inwardly he smacked his forehead at the inane comment so close on the heels of his tender thoughts for a stranger.

"She sounds like a smart woman," he heard Julie whisper as Ginger nuzzled against her cheek. Diego paused and looked up at Julie curiously, but he could see the woman was enraptured with the horse, scratching at the mare's ears as if they'd been lifelong pals. If she was manipulative and calculating, she was really good at it. Once again, Diego compared her to Patti, the last woman he'd known. Julie was on the opposite end of the spectrum in every capacity. He shrugged and settled down to business.

"Come on, I've got to get the snowmobile out. I'll need to slide it out of here and then start it outside."

He leaned over the vehicle and began pushing it out the double doors when Julie quickly came up and pushed from behind.

"Let me help. Do you think Ginger could go with us to check on the cows?"

"She'd sure love to, but the snow is already so deep, and I've got to find all of the females out there. It's quicker right now to saddle this up than to try and get Ginger to feel her way in the snow."

"Oh, I guess I didn't think about how hard it could be for a horse in this kind of snow. I guess I just thought that their legs are so long and all." She turned back to Ginger and breathed in the horsey smell that unearthed primitive memories in any person's soul who moved that close to those creatures.

Diego looked intently at Julie. "You'll get to spend more time with that horse, don't you worry."

***

Julie smiled at his understanding for her sudden passion for the four legged creature. Never in her life had Julie understood what horses meant to men who worked the land, but she suddenly knew that there was a bond that was forged between them that relied on trust and understanding. That was something she had lost too recently, and that was why she was suddenly in love with Ginger. Within minutes, Ginger had given Julie the knowledge that she had a kindred spirit. Julie felt herself waking up here at Betty Lee's, but she knew it wasn't just the horse that was doing the waking.

She gazed at the broad back in front of her as she helped him push the snowmobile out of the barn. *He's incredible*, she thought, watching him prime the vehicle. *He's thoughtful and smart and he's spending the day with me. Where was it I thought I needed to go today?* Julie grinned to herself and waited as Diego climbed on and started the snowmobile.

"Hop on." Diego waved his hand at the back of the seat. Julie climbed on behind him and he revved the engine, spewing snow out the back as Julie yelped with delight, throwing her arms around his middle in order to keep her seat. Her laugh rang out over the roar of the snowmobile.

Down a small ravine and sheltered from the wind were the pigs. As they rode closer, Julie wrinkled her nose at the smell.

"What is that horrible smell?" Julie covered her nose with her gloved hand.

"Those are the pigs!" Diego laughed. "Oh, it gets worse, believe me. That's why they're in this ravine. It keeps them pretty sheltered from the wind and keeps the smell down away from the house!" Julie pulled her scarf up and tucked her chin into the zipper of the jacket. Diego snickered. "You should smell it when the snow melts!"

Julie's eyes began to water as she nudged Diego's shoulder. "How can you stand that?"

"You get used to it."

They pulled up next to the pens and Diego went to feed the monster porkers. Julie followed him and realized the smallest was as large as a German Shepard. The largest was almost as tall as her hips. She stood on a cinder block and watched him scratch the nose of a large black and white pig.

"This is Pepper." He said as he gave an extra handful

of sweet feed. "She's been around for a long time."

"She's huge!" Julie stumbled a little on the block and caught her balance against the fence.

"Careful, now, you don't want to fall in there. She's not so nice with strangers."

"Will you eat her?"

"Nah, not this one. She's a brood sow. She's been like a watchdog for a lot of years, and she's been the mama of several generations of county fair winners. Instead, we keep her happy and clean and fed." He scratched Pepper under the chin fondly and walked the perimeter of the pen, checking for damage.

"The dogs are always out here trying to dig under this wall. I'm not sure if they want to play with the pigs or eat them."

"What if one of the dogs did get in there?"

"The pigs would probably eat it."

Julie gasped, horrified. "Really?"

"Sure, but that's why we don't let them get in." Diego grinned and Julie felt momentarily foolish. Obviously, Diego had things under control, and he probably had for a really long time. She was just a tenderfoot here.

Stepping off the cinder block, she peered through the slats, watching the pigs rut each other out of place at the feeding trough. Finally Diego was ready to move on and Julie was grateful. She had grown accustomed to the smell a bit, but was glad for fresh air deep in her lungs. Pigs were cute and cuddly only as long as they were cartoon characters. They weren't so cute in person, Julie decided.

"What did you think?" Diego brushed his hands

together to clean the snow off his gloves.

"I'm not so sure how I feel about pigs. They sure aren't really like what I thought I knew from books and stuff." The cute little images of housepigs and sows that had befriended dogs from Facebook were a far cry from this reality.

He laughed. "Yeah, they aren't really like Wilbur in Charlotte's Web. Pigs are very friendly, and they even wag their tails when I go out to feed them, but they can be pretty mean, too. You just have to keep an eye on them."

Julie nodded and jumped when a ruckus broke out in the pen.

"Look," Diego leaned over the side. "They're playing." Julie climbed back up on the block to watch two of the pigs play what looked like tag.

She laughed, but slipped again, leaning heavily into Diego, who pulled her tight into his waist to help her reclaim her balance.

"You alright?" She gazed up at him, flushed. She knew her face was red with wind and cold and she felt vulnerable and small. Her face reddened further and she ducked her head as she regained her foothold. He took her hand and led her back to the snowmobile.

The two clambered back on the snowmobile and Diego gunned it south parallel to the mountains that rose above them majestically in their early morning splendor. Julie could imagine what a sunset would look like over those purple giants, but right now, fog, flakes, and clouds interfered with her vision.

Before long, the two came upon the barnlike awning

that was walled in on two sides. Large bales of hay stacked several stories high towered above Julie as she climbed off the snowmobile behind Diego. Sheltered next to them were several cows with their young, many munching on the sides of the bales of hay.

Diego cut down several bales and spread the hay amongst the cattle, and Julie gained enough confidence to follow him. Suddenly, she felt a bump on her back and turned to face the largest set of horns she'd ever seen in her life. She froze, terrified as she faced down a giant black cow.

"Now, Jessica, don't go and frighten the woman," Diego chuckled as he stepped in front of Julie and chucked the horned cow under the chin.

Julie raced to the hay bales and climbed as high as she could while Diego contentedly scratched the monster's nose. Diego's laugh rang out as he watched her zigzag up the stacks. "J-J-Jessica?" She questioned as she shivered from three layers up in the hay bales.

"Yep. This here, is Jessica. My daddy gave her to me when I was a youngster." Julie's eyes were dinner plates in her face and Diego laughed again.

"That monster?" She shivered in fear.

"Aww, she's a little puppy dog, or at least, she thinks so. She's been pretty spoiled all her life." Diego patted the giant animal's neck. "She's always gotten what she wants." Diego scratched Jessica's nose in between the enormous set of horns that Julie thought could do major damage if she had been antagonized.

"So let me get this straight." Julie's voice shook as she took in the sight of the man and his horned pet.

"You keep giant pigs and giant bulls as pets?" She shook her head and trembled in her snow clothes.

Diego chuckled again. "I never really thought of it that way." He slapped Jessica on the flank and turned back to Julie.

"But Jessica isn't a bull. She's a longhorn female, who also happens to be one of the biggest we have. We keep our bulls separate in another field and I either sell them off or decide which will make good breeding stock. Of course, some we also eat. I have a friend who likes to take them to some of the rodeos. They pay off their room and board that way." Jessica rambled off to nudge a young female. "Most bulls are not nice animals. Just like a lot of pigs. It's like dogs. It depends on how you raise them. If you are mean and nasty to them, then they will be in return. On the flip side, if you ignore them or neglect them, then they will behave as nature allows. Jessica and Pepper, and even Ginger had a very different upbringing." He helped Julie down off the bales of hay. She was glad he held it a bit longer than necessary.

"Hey, let me show you something!" He was childlike in his excitement and Julie giggled at the image he made.

"I had a new cow tank put out here a year or two ago in the event of a bad storm like this. It's heated so the trough won't be a brick of ice!" Julie saw the flash of pride in the raised eyebrows and easy smile on Diego's face as he surveyed his handiwork. "My last bull, Junior, won several contests in Las Vegas, so he brought a pretty price. That helped get some stuff done around here."

Julie looked at him without really understanding how the bull brought in a lot of money or where, but suddenly she didn't care. She couldn't deny the enormous crush on this man that grew with every passing moment. She didn't understand how it could happen so fast, but she felt like if she analyzed it, it would disappear, like so many other things in her life.

"Was Junior, Jessica Junior?" She asked to distract herself.

Diego chuckled his throaty laugh. "He sure was. He's actually Pete Junior. He was quite a bit more irritable than Old Pete, who was a champion bucking bull. Pete and Jessica made quite a pair." He pointed to the edge of the awning where a smaller cow stood half in the snow. "That one over there is another of theirs. She's ornery enough to be a bull herself, though not all buckers are just grumpy. Some just like to buck. They like the spirit of the game."

"Do you breed her too?"

"She's a little young still, but I think she'll be ready this summer. She is mean, though, so I haven't decided if she's the right fit."

"So you have a bull named Pete and a cow named Jessica, and they've produced top bull and cow babies that you sell for profit. Is that how it works?"

"Pete Junior took on some of the top bullriders in the world in Las Vegas. That made him pretty valuable. It gave me a chance to sustain my ranch. Pete has quite a reputation, but he's getting old. Pete's cagey and a lot of his offspring don't always turn out to be good roughstock." Julie realized he was saying a lot, but not all of it. She didn't press.

Diego gazed at the herd of cattle in front of him and realized that while most were under the awning together, several were still missing.

"We'll have to go try and track the others down," he said to Julie as she watched him from the bales of hay. "They're probably fine, but with this snow and wind, I'd rather they all were closer together."

"Once we find them, how will we get them here?" Julie quickly looked up at Diego. "Don't tell me they'll just follow you."

He grinned, showing his strong white teeth. "No, they won't just follow. They aren't hard to manipulate, though. We'll just show them the right path back by using the snowmobile to guide them."

Although she was getting colder by the second, Julie was enraptured by the way the plains constantly shifted as Diego drove her across the snow. One minute they were in wide open prairie and the next they were ensconced in a grove of junipers. From years of practice, Diego drove them through the trees and across the hills, farther and farther back on the property. Off to the west the Manzano Mountains rose, while off to the east the plains beckoned. Julie felt small and insignificant out on the land, but not threatened by it. Instead, it made her feel at home, wrapped in the arms of the land. She sighed and unconsciously tightened her arms around Diego's waist.

Diego must have noticed the tightening pressure because he looked down and then over his shoulder at her.

"That's why they call it the land of enchantment," he shouted.

"Hmm? What's that?" Julie turned her head back to Diego.

"It's beautiful, isn't it?" Diego swept his arm to take in the wandering prairie and towering mountains. "I can't imagine living anywhere else."

"It is beautiful." She spoke loudly to be heard over the roar of the snowmobile. "This land suits you. I couldn't imagine you in any other place!" Julie ducked her head behind his shoulder again, shielding her face from the wind and snow. That thought was replaced with ideas of her departure, and the growing doubts about whether she ever wanted to. She'd only been here a day, but already she was a changed woman. The land, the people, the man who sat in front of her, she had never found this level of comfort and apparent stability anywhere in her life. Once her parents had died and she married Adam, she thought she'd come close, but Adam hadn't turned out to be such a great choice. She had lived stifled in apartments all her life in the city. She'd never experienced this sort of space and freedom. It was beginning to consume her and she loved the feeling. It certainly was funny to think about, and she almost giggled aloud. She felt more stability with a man she had just met, than with the man she had made love to for over six years.

Julie's reverie was broken as she felt Diego's posture stiffen abruptly. His body jerked and she half thought he might be having a seizure, but then he turned the snowmobile sharply west and gunned the engine. Julie's fears of having to try CPR were quickly replaced by the image in her mind of being thrown from the vehicle by his sudden erratic driving.

"Hold on!" he shouted as he half stood in the seat.

She straightened quickly and grabbed him more tightly as the snowmobile leapt over the snow, chewing a new path in the still falling flakes.

"Dammit!" Diego shouted and raced as fast as he could across the drifts. He pointed at the pack of coyotes in the distance converging on a kneeling cow. Coyotes yipped and Julie's fears of broken arms were replaced by worse thoughts. She had never seen them, but she had heard about the scavengers. Even though she knew they were more afraid of people, wild animals were not things she understood, and she was terrified. Her teeth began chattering, even through all the layers of clothing that kept her warm.

"I'm not sure we can make it in time," Diego growled, pushing the snowmobile even faster toward the pack.

"Is she still alive?" Julie could see the dog-like predators leaping on the cow's back.

"She won't be for long, if we can't break them up." He cursed that he had left his rifle behind at the house. Julie held on for dear life as he crouched over the handlebars, ready to leap off as soon as he got closer to the cow.

She heard the low moan of the cow as it fell to the ground under the weight of the coyotes. Three hung like burrs off her shoulders and heaving ribcage as the snowmobile roared upon the bloody fight. Julie panicked but released Diego as he leapt off the snowmobile to enter the fracas. The dogs leapt at him, frenzied with the smell and taste of blood on their jaws. Diego kicked at the coyotes who hung on to the cow lowing at him from beneath the pile. Finally two trotted off to the edge of the pasture, but a third growled menacingly and latched his teeth on the throat of the red cow who moaned and dropped her head to the ground. Diego yelled and kicked at the remaining coyote who refused to give up his claim on the downed cow.

"Diego!" Julie screamed as she watched the coyote leap at him, snarling and barking at the rancher.

Diego turned quickly and punched at the coyote at the last minute, and the dog yelped and trotted off to join the others who watched from the treeline. Julie watched them as they prowled menacingly for a moment, then drifted into the cover of the junipers and scrub, vanishing almost without a trace.

Glancing after them, Diego stripped his jacket and unbuttoned his overalls, taking off his overshirt. He piled his clothes off to the side and knelt next to the bleeding cow. "Maybe I can still rescue the calf," he called to Julie who gingerly climbed off the four-wheeler.

"Is the cow still alive?" She asked timidly as she watched in amazement as he gently sliced open the belly of the cow to find the womb.

"I guess not." Thinking she might lose the small breakfast she had eaten, Julie raised a hand to her mouth and turned away, but the next thing she heard made her eyes drip tears of relief. A pitiful bleating sounded from the snow where Diego worked, drawing Julie forward. The calf lived: a tiny, weak, rust-colored calf that was the most beautiful thing she had ever seen.

Diego scrubbed the calf with his shirt, drying off most of the muck and bundled him onto Julie's lap. Julie took off her own jacket and snuggled it around the calf as Diego pulled his jacket back on.

"We'd better get him back to the house. It's cold and he needs to eat." He climbed on the snowmobile and revved it up. Julie fell backward as he took off, and quickly grabbed one hand at the calf and one hand at Diego's jacket to keep her seat. Pitifully, the cow nuzzled her hand weakly, looking for some sustenance.

"But, what about the mother cow?" Julie looked over her shoulder as the fallen cow shrunk in the distance.

"She's gone. I'll call John and Frank to take care of her. They live at the back of the property and manage the cattle on the back end of the property. I might have to have them take a run around the edge to find the rest of the cattle, too."

"Will the coyotes come back?" Julie craned her head around to look at the cow once more, but she could only see a dark spot in the snow.

"Most likely." Diego trained his eyes forward, but shouted over his shoulder. "Coyotes typically only scavenge, but it's a very cold storm, and they must be getting hungry. And brave. We need to get her cleaned up so they don't come back in and threaten the rest of the herd." He shifted gears as the snowmobile bounced over a small incline in the snow. Julie's head bobbed as they hit and she huddled over the calf that sprawled on her legs and behind Diego on the snowmobile.

"Good thing they weren't wolves. We'd have real problems then," he continued grimly.

"W-wolves?"

"Not anything for you to be frightened of. Coyotes are bad enough." He revved the snowmobile over a bank of snow and the house came into sight. "Are you hungry?"

Julie groaned and clutched her stomach. "You want me to eat after watching that?"

"What? Oh," Diego ducked his head. "Yeah, sorry. That was probably not something you're used to seeing."

"And you are?"

"Well, it has to happen sometimes. I mean, it's a ranch in the middle of a wide open prairie. Nature exists and those things must happen."

Julie composed herself, though she felt weak and pale. She figured that by now there was no blood left in her head, but she understood that the nature of the circumstances required that heroics were in order. From her estimation, Diego had risen to the situation admirably. Maybe she was becoming a little bit biased as far as how interesting he was becoming. She shook her head and looked down at the calf. Adam would never have done this. He wouldn't have allowed his hands to get covered in blood. And to fight off a pack of coyotes? Adam's idea of bravery was picking up the remote. Diego was blowing her mind.

Chapter Eleven

"We better get him warmed up and fed soon, or he won't make it. I can't quite believe he's still with us, honestly." Julie watched Diego pick up the calf and take him into the kitchen.

Julie didn't know what to do, so she just stood in the doorway and listened to Diego as he settled the calf down in the corner near the woodstove. He quickly stoked the fire and before long it was emitting heat and warming the corner of the kitchen.

"Hey, Julie, why don't you come sit over here on the floor by this guy," Diego softly urged, taking her by the hand as she hesitantly stepped closer. She'd just held the calf in her lap for the past fifteen minutes, but she wasn't sure what to do now. Blood was still moist on the front of her snowpants as she gazed at the helpless calf. He struggled to stand, weak and tired from his chaotic birth.

"I'll get some powder out of the barn."

"What are you getting?" Julie heard the question squeak out as she reached a hand out to touch the soft blowing nose of the calf.

"Early cow's milk formula. It's the first milk and a calf needs that to be healthy.

"You keep that around?" Julie half gasped, forgetting that she was on a ranch, and that was something many ranchers probably did in case something crazy like a random calving in front of raving coyotes happened again, because you never can be sure...Julie's mind whirled. She felt like she was in the Twilight Zone. Witnessing the calf's birth had to have been one of the most unique and vivid experiences of her life. She wasn't sure how to think about it.

"Sure! We keep powdered formula on hand in case an animal is rejected, or something like this happens," but he was quick to add, "which isn't often."

"Why do you think the coyotes attacked that cow?" Julie collected herself and sat down on the floor next to the calf. She quickly stood back up and looked around for towels, but Diego had beaten her to it and stepped back into the room with a handful of old towels from the linen closet in the hall.

"I don't know. I have the feeling she was close to birthing and was weak. I noticed the tracks of several other cattle, so I imagine they were all together and became spooked by the coyotes. She must have fallen behind." He dampened a towel in warm water and washed the muzzle of the little calf. "I need to call the guys and have them take a look at her and take care of her. If there is anything left." He grimaced. "I have the feeling the calf just used up all she had. She probably was so weak that she got separated, and then started to give birth and the coyotes came out." He knelt next to Julie and helped her clean the almost dried calf. "Here, I'll get some hot water." He stood and filled a basin in the sink. "I've seen it sometimes. The calf takes all of her nutrients and her blood poisons her as it nourishes him. Usually it kills both of them. I think this time it was probably a combination of a lot of things."

Diego handed Julie a moist towel as she handed him a soiled one.

"I can't quite believe we got there in time to save him, and even though he's here and breathing, I'm not sure he'll make it. He doesn't look good." Diego eyed the calf skeptically.

"Maybe if we feed him, he'll perk up." Julie took a dry towel and rubbed the calf's newly cleaned coat dry. "Yep," she murmured, "I think he'll make it."

***

Diego thought about the determination Julie showed with the calf. He wondered how she would react if the calf didn't make it. He was curious. He was impressed. He wondered where her quiet strength seemed to surge from. Julie often seemed too meek and gentle to be so strong, but then she would say or do something to surprise him. He always had liked surprises.

He watched as the calf was stretched up to nuzzle Julie's chin. She wasn't fighting it too hard, the grin on her face clearly indicating exactly how she felt.

"It's a shame we lost the mother. She was just a little heifer. This was her first. It's too bad."

"Is this Junior's baby too?"

"Actually, I think this might be another bull's. We had them separated differently earlier in the spring. It's bad breeding timing on our part." He stood and rinsed the towel. "I think this might be Mustard's. He's a big yellow bull. He tears cowboys up in the ring. That's a bull who is an athlete."

"Are you going to try and put this baby with another cow?"

"I'd like to. He needs to be raised in the fields, not in the house. Let me show you how to feed him out of a bottle and then I have to go get some firewood."

"He's exhausted." He rose to his feet and started the preparation.

"Come on, little guy, you have to make it. We're going to get you some food and then you can get strong and smart." Julie rubbed her fingers over the calf's mouth and gasped as he started to suckle her finger. She giggled. "You won't get any milk out of that, silly. Just hang on, Diego will be right back with some good stuff." Julie let the calf suckle her finger and with her other hand stroked his side. The calf had given up trying to stand, and rested quietly next to the woodstove, his head in Julie's lap.

Diego worked efficiently then knelt next to Julie and the calf. He chuckled when he saw the calf nursing Julie's finger and replaced that with the nipple of the bottle.

"Here, just hold his neck firmly like this and hold the bottle like you would for a baby." He cradled the calf between his arms and his lap, holding the calf's neck firmly with one arm and the bottle with his other hand. "Once he figures out he's feeling better, he'll try to get up again. Sometimes they get lazy like this." Diego watched Julie take the bottle and situate herself as he suggested.

"Will he be okay?"

"I bet he'll be fine. He seems to be pretty eager to drink that. He's had a rough morning." Diego pushed a lock of hair out of Julie's face as he watched her mother the calf.

Julie looked up at him and smiled. "What will we do with him after he eats? Is he going to stay in here?"

"Nah, we'll take him out to see if one of the cows will take him and if not, we'll see what Ginger has to say about it. It shouldn't be a problem. Besides, Natalie will definitely take him in if the others don't. She's as much a softie as Ginger."

The two looked at each other as the calf nursed the bottle. The warmth from the woodstove and the peace in the kitchen had sedated both Julie and Diego. Once the calf drained the bottle, he didn't fall asleep. Instead, he wobbled to his feet and began nosing around the kitchen. Julie didn't move and neither did Diego. The two were drawn together in a quiet intimacy. Diego gazed into Julie's eyes and itched to draw her into his arms.

Julie's hand strayed to his cheek and caressed it softly.

"When that coyote jumped at you, I was so worried. I thought you were going to be hurt."

Her eyes glowed in the dimly lit room and Diego grasped her hand gently. He turned his face and kissed the palm of Julie's hand and said, "I wasn't in any danger. They are more afraid of us than we are of them. That coyote was just hungry."

"Yeah, but," she started to protest and Diego pulled

her into an embrace.

"You were worried about me, weren't you," he teased.

"Well, actually, I don't know how to drive a snowmobile, so I wasn't sure how I was going to get all of us back here," she teased back.

"Oh really," Diego growled and started to tickle her sides. "I guess I'll just have to teach you, then."

"Diego!" Julie laughed breathlessly, "Diego, stop! I can't breathe" she giggled.

Mercilessly Diego continued until Julie was on the ground, Diego straddled on top of her, smirking down at her helpless state.

"Tell me you cared," he demanded jestfully.

"I-ok, ok! I, yes, I did. I do," she breathed, her giggles quieting, her eyes deepening in color as the look between them intensified.

Suddenly a crash sounded by the sink and the two jumped up to see the calf bouncing backwards from the pans that hit the floor.

"I guess he feels better," Julie laughed as Diego ran around the table to catch the frantic calf.

"Yep, I guess so. Maybe we should try and hook him up with a new mama before he gets into any more mischief."

Julie looked down at her soiled snow pants and shrugged. "Maybe I should change, first."

Diego eyed her up and down and shook his head.

"You look beautiful, muck and all. Besides, we still have to get firewood, remember?" he teased.

"Right. What about the calf, though?" She gestured at

the kitchen, taking the pots and pans on the floor and the restless calf in with the sweep of her arm.

Diego laughed as he took in the same scene. "I think he'll be okay. We just need to refill the woodbox here and in the living room." Shaking his head, he said, "There isn't much more damage he can do in here, and I don't think he'll go far."

"Okay, boss, lead on." She saluted and grabbed her jacket.

Chapter Twelve

"Hey y'all! We're back! Come look at the tree we found!" Natalie's voice rang out through the house, pulling Julie back to reality.

She had once again become sedated and lazy sitting on the floor in the kitchen by the woodstove. The wood pile was replenished, she had a half a cup of hot coffee and the calf was licking her leg as if it was the most natural thing in the world to do.

"Nino! You should see the tree!" Aidan's tiny voice rang out from the foyer and Diego pulled Julie up to go meet them in the next room.

"It means uncle," he murmured, as two bundles of snowsuits, hats and mittens launched themselves at Diego's knees.

"Hey guys," he chuckled as he grabbed both the children up in his arms and whirled them around the living room.

"Come on guys, get back over here" Gabe called to his children. "You need to get those snowsuits off before you start dripping all over the floor."

"Diego, help Gabe get that tree in here." Natalie stripped her hat and gloves off and stamped her feet in the foyer. "It's beautiful, just wait until you see it," she said to Julie breathlessly.

Julie smiled at Natalie and took her hat and gloves as Natalie unzipped her parka.

"I can't believe it is still snowing out there!"

"I know, we went out earlier to check on the cattle. I can't quite believe it, either!" Julie grinned, "Hey Natalie, come in the kitchen, let me show you something." The kids clamored at Diego as Julie led Natalie into the kitchen to meet the latest addition to the family.

The rust colored calf was sprawled in front of the woodstove, gazing mournfully up at the two women who promised to help him stand up.

"Oh, what a sweetie!" Natalie took in the empty bottles in the sink and knelt to hug the new calf. She looked up at Julie and asked, "what happened to his mother?"

"Diego rescued him from coyotes." Julie shuddered at the memory and knelt to pet the soft curls of the new calf. "He says we have to try and see if one of the cows will take him, and if not, he wants to try Ginger." Julie went on to relate the story of Diego's coyote attack and calf rescue.

Natalie looked curiously at Julie. "You've gotten a good taste of the ranch today, haven't you?"

Julie laughed. "Boy, have I. I've never done so many new things in one day in my life!" She looked down at the muddy sweater she wore. "I'm sorry I ruined this sweater."

Natalie laughed. "You didn't ruin it. It's just mud. I'm glad it fit!"

Shyly, Julie smiled. "Thank you for leaving the warm clothes for me. It was an amazing adventure today." Natalie nodded and braced herself as she heard her kids crashing down the hall toward them. They raced into the kitchen, Diego and Gabe close behind.

"Oh, he's so cute!"

"Alright!" Aidan shrieked. "I was hoping we'd have a new calf this year!" Natalie's youngest turned to his mom. "Can we keep him inside this time?" He looked pleadingly at his mother and turned to his father and Diego. "Please? Can we?"

Alexandra chimed in. "Please can we keep him inside this year? Please?" Both kids were clamoring at their parents and their uncle, and the calf nervously stood and hid behind Julie's leg.

Diego laughed. "Come on guys, let's go in the other room. We're getting him all worked up. He can stay inside for now, but he needs to go out with the others in a little bit."

"Awww," the kids chorused, clearly distressed that they were going to lose another house pet. Julie grinned and stroked the calf's neck. Natalie turned to the kids and shooed them out of the room, at the same time muttering about getting dinner ready. Gabe distracted the kids with ideas of decorating the tree.

"I get to put the star on this year!"

"You got to do it last year!" The two argued as they went with their father. The three of them wandered off to find the boxes of ornaments that were in the attic.

Natalie turned to Diego and Julie. "Have you eaten yet?" She asked the two. Julie was astonished at how

Natalie could think about others when she had just come in from an all morning adventure out in the cold. Julie thought she'd fall into a heap on the sofa, exhausted, especially with two rambunctious kids.

"Nope, not yet." Diego replied as he turned on the faucet to wash his hands. "We were just about to, but wanted to get some firewood in first."

"Well, let me make up something warm. I know the kids are hungry too, even though they are a little distracted with ornaments right now." Natalie began to putter around the kitchen, pulling items out of cupboards and the pantry.

"Can I help with anything?" Julie asked, trying to feel a little less useless.

"Oh, no, honey. You just go get cleaned up. You look full of mud!"

"I think we still have to get that calf out to the barn." She looked at Diego. "Is that what we're doing?"

Julie sat on the floor near the woodstove where she and Diego had been sitting earlier. The calf tottered over and collapsed in her lap. She giggled and the calf nudged her hand, looking for more food.

"I think he's still hungry."

"Probably. I'll go get some more milk for him." Diego pulled his jacket back on. "At this rate, he'll be ready to go out to the pasture before long!"

Natalie watched the exchange and smiled to herself. *It's about time Diego met a woman who warmed him like that.*

Chapter Thirteen

After lunch, Natalie took Julie on a tour of the house.

"We didn't get a chance last night, so now I'll show you around!" Natalie proudly pointed out the antique buffet and walnut dining set that had belonged to her great-great-grandparents. She insisted they had been brought across the ocean and then across the country in a wagon train, finally to reside in this house.

"Betty Lee was my great-great-grandmother. She met my great-great-grandfather after her trip west in a buckboard with her parents. They set up a ranch here after several months of difficult travel." Natalie caressed the back of a dining chair lovingly. "The ranch used to be so much larger, but over the years, it's been parceled out to family members and to pay off debts, especially during the Depression, but this house has remained mostly the same." She grinned. "Except, of course, for the addition of plumbing and electricity!"

The dining room was spacious, much like the rest of the house, decorated in a simple country style that spoke to Julie of comfort and utility. In here, too, the adobe bricks were exposed, and thick wooden beams accented the framework. The effect was impressive, yet continued to convey a sense of homelike security.

"I love how comfortable this place is. I feel so at home here." Julie stroked her hand along the chair rail that had been burnished smooth by years of use.

"It's comfy, alright. When Gabe and I moved in with Diego, I always thought that we'd feel cramped, but once we were settled, it's like the house was designed for exactly the way we live. And there are plenty of rooms. Diego's quarters in the back make it seem more like two connected houses, rather than trying to put all of us together."

"What made you decide to turn this into a Bed and Breakfast?"

"We just had so much room, and even though Diego inherited the lion's share of the property and the buildings, he never really wanted to be in them alone. He loves the kids as much as if they were his own." She sighed and glanced sideways at Julie. "He needs to get married and have some kids of his own, but he's just so private. He doesn't like to let people in. Except for that bitch Patti." Natalie reached for the patio door. "Actually," she turned thoughtfully. "I'm not so sure anymore that he actually did let her into his heart." She pulled the door open and gestured to Julie to enter the outdoor room first. "I just am so glad he dumped her. She was a piece of work, that's for sure."

Julie looked questioningly at Natalie, surprised that she would share such private information about her brother, but intrigued, nonetheless. She said nothing, hoping Natalie would share more about this woman Diego had possibly loved.

"He sure seems to have taken a liking to you, that's for sure."

Julie's face flushed, and her toes felt like they had curled in her shoes. "Uh, well, he's a really great guy," She stammered, memories of his body straddling hers as he tickled her earlier in the day crowding out everything else.

Natalie laughed. "Yes, he's a really great guy. We know that." She winked at Julie. "He's also single." Playfully, she nudged Julie's shoulder.

Julie grinned. "He's also very attractive, I'll admit that, too." Her face, already red, was surely the shade of Natalie's sweater.

"Uh huh. He's good looking too. Looks just like me." Natalie put her arm around Julie and they walked out onto the patio together.

If Julie's face could turn any darker red, she'd have probably fainted.

The closed patio was dreamlike in its simplicity. Snow still fell, giving it a fairy tale appearance, with inches of snow covering the decorative bushes and flowerbeds. The adobe walls created a setting fit for a princess. To the back was a hot tub in a simple gazebo of southwest design. There were symmetrical pine trees in all four corners, and off to the side was a natural rock fountain. On one side was a giant leafless Cottonwood that in the summer would shade the patio from the afternoon sun. Today she saw that the trunk and halfway up the branches were white Christmas lights, though she would have to wait until sunset to see the effect they had on the aesthetics of the enclosure.

"Out here, we have barbecues and parties, and sometimes we'll get a wedding party in the spring."

"It's lovely."

Julie gazed at the glittering snowflakes that continued to fall, thinking about the romance of the patio, imagining some young woman preparing to marry the love of her life. She thought of her own failed marriage, but tried to resist the desperation it raised in the back of her throat. This place was too beautiful to remember such pain.

"I bet this waterfall is incredible when the water is flowing over it." Julie gestured at the artistic statement of water and earth that anchored the patio to the houses that surrounded it.

"Diego built that fountain out of boulders that he found at the back of the property." Natalie's words brought her back to the present. She brushed snow off one side of the fountain and exposed the red of the stone that glowed in the setting sunlight. "He hauled that big base stone out of the face of the cliff at the back of the property and the others he found near that same area. Don't you think it is the most beautiful thing you've ever seen?"

"Wow. He made this?" Julie moved closer to get a better look at the structure that was still in the freezing air. Icicles dripped from the rock formation, giving it a jagged appearance and adding to its natural beauty. The stones were stacked to resemble a cliff with a waterfall surging down the middle. It looked just like the images Julie had seen of incredible waterfalls in

South America. She could see it sparkling in her mind, the pleasant chatter of the water falling over the levels of rock. She imagined sitting here and listening to it while the children played around it.

"He made it for my mom just before she died. She and my father were in a car accident on the mountain several years ago."

"Oh, I'm sorry. I had no idea." Julie turned to see Natalie's shuttered anguish.

"We all miss them. They were the glue in this family, definitely. Diego took it especially hard. He had hoped to run the ranch with my dad for many more years." She smiled sadly. We actually have another brother, but he and his wife live in Texas. Jake's wife, actually, disagreed about some things Diego did with the property after my parents died, so we haven't talked to them much in the last couple of years."

"Jake is your brother?"

"He is. He's our younger brother, and he's been married to this woman who is the biggest pain in the neck you've ever met. All she cares about is how big her diamond is and how much she can spend in a day."

"Oh." Julie didn't really know what to say. Natalie's pain was similar to what Julie had known in losing her parents, but so different, too. Her own mother had died of ovarian cancer some years before, and her father had followed not long after. He had loved his wife so completely that he couldn't bear the thought of living without her. Julie had learned the art of love from two masters, and she despaired of ever attaining the same great love that her parents had known. She had never had siblings, so she didn't even know what disagreeing with one about inheritance decisions would look like.

"Brr, it's cold out here." Natalie shivered and smiled brightly, recovering from her momentary sadness. "Let's go back in and make hot chocolate."

"That sounds fun, but I need to take a bath first. It's been a really long day. But hot chocolate sounds like it would hit the spot!"

"Perfect. I'll get the kids decorating, and when you come down, we can all drink hot cocoa and sit by the fire." She moved to open the door and turned back to Julie in excitement. "Ooh, and we can add some Irish Crème!" Natalie giggled like a child at the thought of tucking in with some booze. Julie couldn't help but grin in response.

"I'd love that. I'll hurry."

"No, darlin', you just take your time. We've got all night to get to know each other!"

The idea of girl time was suddenly super appealing to Julie and it made her wonder why she'd never had a stronger circle of female friends. She was going to change that when she got back. Maybe she'd even forgive Sara.

Chapter Fourteen

Downstairs, a cacophony was brewing. Kids were arguing over who would put up which ornament, Natalie and Gabe were arguing vigorously about whether to put tinsel on or not, and Diego was stoking the fire, which already roared with a vibrant heat and crackle. It was impossible not to enjoy the moment, and sneak as she might, she could not escape the notice of everyone as she strolled down the stairs.

"Julie, tell Gabe that tinsel is not a standard Christmas decoration!"

"It most certainly is!"

"Come on, Mom! Just let dad put that stuff on the tree!"

"Yeah, come on, Mom." Diego added to the frackas.

"Do I need to get involved in this?" Julie's grin split from ear to ear. She was thrilled to be in the midst of the battle. She curled her feet under her as she sat comfortably on the sofa and watched them all engage. Presently forgotten, she watched the family, amused.

Julie gazed at Diego in the firelight. Her bath had relaxed her, but thoughts of Adam lingered in her brain, almost forcing her to make comparisons to the first man who had turned her head in years. Diego was tall, where Adam was only an inch or two taller than Julie's own five feet, four inches. Diego was dark haired with the most intensely blue eyes she'd ever seen, where Adam was light haired and his eyes were a watery blue. Diego had a straight white smile that lit up his whole face, while Adam had a smile that was always forced and also a little fake. His vanity had him in the dentist's chair four times a year getting a fresh bleaching. Adam's hands were manicured and soft, while Diego's were strong, callused, and made Julie weak to think about how they would feel on her skin. She flushed as she watched him help Aidan put ornaments on branches the little boy couldn't reach. He turned as if he felt her eyes on him and smiled into her soul. She about melted into the sofa with that look.

Natalie handed a mug of cocoa to Julie and then sat next to her on the sofa by the fire. "So what do you think?"

Julie physically pulled herself from her thoughts with a shiver. She forced herself to concentrate on what Natalie was saying. Given their earlier conversation, Julie couldn't help but wonder if Natalie meant Diego. She almost commented on the shape of his rear in those jeans, but she refrained as she realized Natalie meant the entire atmosphere.

"This is so much fun," Julie laughed. "Your kids are having a great time with this tree. You chose a lovely one for this house."

"It's our favorite time of year! We looked

everywhere for that tree this morning." She took a sip of her cocoa. "Usually we get it up a bit sooner, but this year was just so busy with guests, and this was the first time we've been able to get out to find one. And Gabe insists on that damn tinsel."

"Come on, Mom! You need to put up your ornaments!" Aidan grabbed a hold of Natalie's hand and tugged her away from Julie. Alexandra quickly followed.

"Come on, Julie, you too!" Alexandra chimed.

"Yeah, Julie, you too!" Diego grinned. He handed her a glass bulb and helped Alexandra guide Julie to a bare spot on the tree. Julie smiled at the two of them and hung the ornament on a branch. She stepped back to size up the tree and Diego handed her another ornament, this one a hand-carved wooden horse. It was painted with streaks of red and green, and danced on the ribbon that held it.

"Oh, that's my favorite one!" Natalie peered over Julie's shoulder at the ornament she held. "Diego made that one for our mother several years ago!" Diego smiled shyly at Julie as she looked at him tenderly.

Natalie reached into the box of ornaments and started passing various shapes out to the kids and her husband. "Each of these ornaments has some sort of story behind it. Some of these are as old as we are, and in fact, some of them are even older."

Diego took the one Natalie held in her hand at that moment, another wooden one, this one stained with the passage of time. "This one was carved when my great-grandfather was born." Almost reverently, he placed it high on the tree near the lights so it would shine in the glow.

This ornament was another horse, this one rearing on two legs and pawing at the air. The wood was reddish in color and darkened nicely. Julie thought she had never seen anything so beautiful in all her life. She was envious of the history these people shared. She could only imagine having that kind of heritage to share with her children. Even if she and Adam had produced a child, there wouldn't have been this kind of history. Julie hardly knew anything about Adam's past, and she didn't have much to share, either. Her parents loved her so much, but both had also been only children. Even the fact that Julie had been born had been a surprise to her parents, because neither thought they could have children.

Julie felt Diego's eyes upon her as she reminisced. Once again, she was having a conversation with herself, and she sensed his fascination. She stood in the middle of the floor with an old-fashioned Santa in her hand, activity continuing all around her, unsure of how to move forward. She placed the ornament on the tree next to a bulb and stood back, collecting her cocoa.

"This is perfect." She sighed.

"Yeah." Diego stood beside her again, watching the others.

"It would be even better with tinsel." Gabe moaned from his ladder as he rearranged the star on the top of the tree.

Chapter Fifteen

It was getting late, and the kids were settling into the bedtime routine upstairs with Natalie and Gabe. The murmurs from upstairs and the crackling fire had put both Julie and Diego into a relaxed mood. Diego had entertained the kids for hours with stories and sketches of the old west and the calf had seamlessly entered the nighttime routine. He never did make it out to the barn.

Julie had settled in front of the fire, the calf resting peacefully across her lap, her head nestled on the seat of the couch. She gazed at the beams that protruded from the ceiling, giving the living room its country cabin characteristic.

"This really is a beautiful home. You were very lucky to grow up in such a place." She turned her head to gaze at Diego as he worked on the art pad in front of him.

He paused and looked back at her, his eyes lidded and heavy with the soft tension that was building in the room. "I was very lucky. I had a great upbringing, and I have a wonderful family." He looked back down at what he was working on. "It is a quiet life, but it is a beautiful one, and I'm grateful for it every single day." He paused to smudge the pencil a bit on the page. "What about you, Julie? What was it like for you as a child?"

She sighed and looked at the calf that rested in her lap. Tenderly, she stroked the brow of its face. "Oh, it was a city upbringing, you know, we lived in an apartment, we'd visit the park after school and take drives on the weekend. My parents were wonderful, but they died a few years ago."

"No sisters or brothers to keep you occupied?"

"Nope. Just me. My parents never even thought they would be able to have a child, and I was a surprise later in life for them. My mother was 42 when she had me."

"Wow, I imagine that wasn't always easy. My parents were young when they married and had us pretty quickly, and we are each only about a year apart. They used to joke that they had to get cable or they would have had ten of us."

Julie giggled, imagining the happy humor of Diego's family. Obviously, his parents had done something right to have such an open and heartwarming family.

"You have a brother, too, right?"

Diego's grin changed to a look of irritation and he snorted. "Yeah, I have a brother. He has chosen to leave the homestead and do something else, though. We hardly see him."

Julie felt awkward and regretted bringing up something that so obviously tortured Diego.

"So what will we do about Snowflake, here?" Julie

extended her hand to the calf that still rested his head on her lap, as if he were a puppy.

"Snowflake? So you've decided that's his name, huh?"

Idly, she stroked the curl that centered on Snowflake's forehead. "I think that's the perfect name for him, considering the circumstances." The calf snorted in his sleep and she smiled. "So tell me, Diego, what are you like?"

Diego looked up from the unfinished sketch in his lap and smiled into Julie's eyes.

"What do you mean, what am I like? What you see is what you get," he growled.

Julie laughed at his tone. "Okay, if what I see is what I get, when can I get it over here?" she flirted. Diego set his pad aside and slid closer to Julie's legs, his hands sliding along her ankles and along her calf up to her knee.

"I'm a simple man, really," he whispered, looking into her eyes and making her spine melt along the sofa.

"I like a good joke, a cold beer and a hot woman, though not always in that order," his hand reached her upper thigh and she gasped as he moved closer and kissed her neck, nipping some skin along the way.

Julie jumped and her head came up as she put her hand out to stop Diego.

"Diego, please don't."

"Julie, I—" He stopped abruptly and moved away from her, running his hand through his hair. "I'm sorry. I shouldn't have pushed you."

"No, I asked for it. I—I—" she reached her hand out

and gently touched his forearm. "I just—It's just that I haven't been with a man other than my ex-husband in years, and—" She sighed, frustrated, not sure why she was pushing him away. Her heart beat fast, making her feel light-headed. Why in the hell was she pushing him away? This man was beautiful, kind, compassionate, gentle, what was she thinking? She wanted him in every corner of her soul, but she was terrified to let him in.

Diego rested his cheek on her head and sighed. "I understand, Julie. I find you very attractive, but I won't push you where you don't want to go. I can't deny that I am attracted to you, though."

"I feel the same." Julie pushed the calf off her lap and moved to stand up. Diego stood up quickly to help her to her feet. "Perhaps I should head for bed. What should we do about the calf?"

"Don't worry about it, you go to bed and I will take care of it." Spontaneously, Diego pulled Julie into a hug and kissed her forehead gently. "Sleep well, Julie."

Chapter Sixteen

Julie sat up with a gasp. Her heart was racing and she strained to hear what it was that woke her up. She didn't hear a thing, but couldn't rest back against the pillows. She stood and tossed her robe over her shoulders. Something wasn't right.

She stepped into the hall and looked around, confused, her heart pounding in her chest. The hall was softly lit by the snowlit night. Julie heard the quiet sounds of night, the creaking of an old house, the restlessness of children sleeping, but she could not identify what it was that had pulled her from her dreams. She stood there, blood pounding through her brain, wondering why she was even out of bed. She hadn't felt this intense sense of concern since her mother had died.

She checked first on Alexandra, but the little girl was

sleeping soundly, the pink ruffled quilt pulled to her chin. Julie moved on to Aidan's room, and as she glanced at the window, she thought she saw a movement near the barn. She stepped closer and stifled a cry as she saw a figure run furtively under the phosphorescent overhead lamp that lit the barnyard. She glanced at Aidan to make sure he still slept soundly and then she flew down the stairs and out the back door.

Not sure what she would do once she confronted a stranger while she herself was a stranger here, she paused. Alarmed, Julie smelled smoke in the air and looked at the barn as she started to run again, not certain what drove her toward Diego's apartment. Her brain raced, and she questioned why she hadn't stopped at Natalie and Gabe's door, but then suddenly she knew. She never noticed the snow filling her half slippers once she saw the flames licking out of the corner of the roof of the barn.

"Diego!" Julie pounded on his door as she frantically looked around for a hose or a bucket. "Diego!" She screamed again.

After what seemed a million years, he opened the door sleepily, his hair cast in awkward directions, his chest gleaming in the moonlight. Julie barely took the time to notice as she gasped out, "Fire! There's a fire in the barn!"

Diego's eyes opened wide and there was no longer a hint of sleep in them.

"Call the fire department and get Natalie and Gabe out here! You go in and stay warm." He launched into action, grabbing his boots and jacket and racing toward the barn.

Julie obeyed as far as waking Natalie and Gabe, but after taking just long enough to pull on her own boots and trading her robe for her warmer coat, she was out the door and at the barn too. Natalie was on the phone with the fire department and Gabe ran out behind her to help.

Snowflake and Ginger were trapped and Julie wasn't going to sit by and let anything happen to them. She heard the horses screaming as she approached the barn. Diego was nowhere to be seen.

He had pulled open the large main doors in the front and as she ran toward the opening, she saw the giant stallion race out the door and into the night. She followed the path he had exited and went to Ginger's stall. The mare was wild eyed with fright, smoke rolling overhead. Snowflake was bawling and cowered in the corner, trying to avoid the striking hooves of the panicked mare. Julie quickly unlatched the stall and Ginger came racing out, biting at the calf to follow. Julie had the presence of mind to get out of the way, but she realized that Snowflake wasn't moving. His panic had terrified him to the point of paralysis. Julie entered the stall; Diego was whistling and shooing the horses out of the barn behind her.

She looked around and noticed Ginger's lead on a hook just outside the stall. She grabbed it and looped it around Snowflake and started to pull, urging him with her gentle voice. He may have been only a day old, but he was already heavy, and he pulled against her. No matter how much he may have trusted her, he was panicked and wasn't moving. Julie went around behind him and gave him a shove, lifting his rear feet off the ground, but he dug in.

"Come on!" she urged as the smoke got worse. Flames had already begun to lick around the edges of the stall when Diego finally realized she was in there. She coughed and tugged, her eyes tearing in the smoke that was engulfing her.

"Julie, get out!" He ran into the stall and grabbed her by the arm, pushing her toward the door, but she turned to plead with him. "Go!" He yelled, panic beginning to strain his voice. He grabbed Snowflake in his arms and barreled through the door and Julie raced ahead of him, eager to be out in the clean air.

The horses were out of sight in the dark, but Ginger nickered for Snowflake and he struggled to be let down. Out of the barn and immediate danger, his sole objective was to reunite with his adopted mother. Diego gladly let him loose and then he gathered Julie in his arms.

"Why did you go in there, you crazy girl?" He murmured against her hair.

"I had to get Ginger and Snowflake out." She pushed against Diego and wrapped her arms around him, his scent obscured by smoke and cinder. She burrowed into his chest and began to cry.

"I would have gotten them out. What if something had happened to you?" He pulled her tighter into his arms and stroked her hair. He rested his cheek against her head as he watched his barn begin to burn in earnest.

Natalie and Gabe stood near them, their arms around one another as they heard fire trucks wailing in the distance.

Julie pulled away abruptly and looked up at Diego.

"I saw someone."

"What? What do you mean?" Diego held her arms while Natalie and Gabe crowded in around the two of them.

"I heard something and went to check on the kids, but as I looked out of Aidan's room, I noticed a figure run under the light here in the yard." She turned to look at all of them. "When I ran to Diego's quarters, I noticed the barn on fire."

"Why, that's crazy!" Natalie scoffed, but a worried crease marred her brow. "You think someone did this on purpose? Who would have set the barn on fire?"

With a crack and a roar, part of the roof caved inward. They all turned to watch the flames grow as one of the walls leaned ominously inward over where the horse stalls were, and where Julie had just been only moments before.

"Oh no," Julie whispered.

Gabe turned to his wife, "You better go check on the kids. See if they're still sleeping. If this fire starts to spread, we need to get out of the house too."

"Right. But in the meantime, I'll get some coffee on." She turned to look at Diego. "You don't think it could have been—no," she shook her head and turned away. "I'll go make coffee. You guys come in when the fire department gets things under control."

Chapter Seventeen

Sheriff Bizzell arrived at the ranch within minutes of the fire truck. Jack Bizzell was country through and through. His mutton chopped mustache and white cowboy hat emphasized his small town pride and his over-sized ego. He spoke to Gabe first, looking around for Diego. Snow began to fall again, soft wet flakes that stuck to his mustache and beaded on his hat.

Diego was standing with Chief Jonas Bradley of the fire department. Diego shared what Julie had told him she had seen. Bradley agreed that he didn't believe that this was an accident.

"From the initial accounts you guys gave us, I have the feeling this was an arson, Diego. You need to be ready for that." Diego shook his head in puzzlement.

"Who would have set my barn on fire?" He ran his hand through his hair and looked for Julie. He finally saw her with Ginger and Snowflake in a small paddock, rubbing her hand through the mare's forelock, her other hand on the calf's head. Snowflake nuzzled his face under the open flap of her jacket and he could see her tenderly coo some words at the farm animal. Diego shook his head again and turned back to Chief Bradley. "I have no idea how this happened, but we need to get to the bottom of it, and fast. It's still snowing, and now the horses have no shelter!" Diego was meticulous in taking care of his stock and machinery, so some of his expensive equipment was stored in the barn that was now raging hotly. Fortunately, he had gotten the stock out, but the four-wheelers and smaller tractors were still inside, probably water-logged and destroyed in the fire.

"I know that. Did you recently put in for more insurance on your barn or property?" Bradley asked as a matter of course, not out of outright suspicion, but unfortunately, Sheriff Bizzell walked up right at that moment.

"Insurance claim, huh?" Bizzell spat blackened tobacco juice into the trampled snow at their feet. "Didja hope to profit off this, huh, Diego?" He tempered his venom with a smile and Diego gritted his teeth in irritation.

"Come on, Sheriff. You know Diego has put his heart and soul into this place, and he wouldn't do anything to destroy it. Besides, he shares it with all of us come summer, even you. You know he didn't do this." Chief

103

Bradley turned his shoulders to stand squarely next to Diego, glaring from under thick black eyebrows at his colleague.

"We just have to cover all the bases, there, Chief, you know that."

"It's fine, Jonas. He's just doing his job." Diego clapped his hand on the shoulder of his childhood friend. "Thanks, buddy. Let's just figure out who did this." He nodded companionably at Jonas and turned back to Sheriff Bizzell. "Tell me what you need to know."

"Who's that woman over there?" He swept his arm in the direction of Julie, who was still in the paddock with the animals.

"Julie Davenport. She's a guest staying with us this week."

"What's she doing here?"

Diego looked at the Sheriff in disbelief. "Well, this *is* a Bed and Breakfast, Sheriff. She's on vacation."

"Do you think it could have been this new woman staying with you guys at the B and B?" The sheriff drawled at Diego, and then spit another sluice of tobacco juice out of the side of his mouth.

"Julie?" Diego scratched his head. "No, I don't think she could have, or would have. She was in the house and ran out to get me." He turned to the barn. "I don't think she would have done this. She said she saw someone running off into the fields." He shook his head.

The sheriff gazed at the flames still licking out of the ribs of the roof. "Uh huh." He nodded suspiciously. "Could she just be saying she saw someone?"

Diego shook his head irritably, his irritation and stress beginning to show through in the face of the sheriff's inane questioning. "I suppose she could be, but I don't think she's going to lie about something like that. She was the first to find the fire, and the first in the barn after me to get the horses out. I don't believe she'd purposely set a fire, then put her life at risk over some horses that belong to a guy she just met." Diego ran his hand through his hair, wishing he'd grabbed a hat before he'd raced out of his house. The snow was falling thickly once again.

"Maybe she did it to get to you, Diego. Didja ever think of that? Women are twisted, ya know." Diego wanted to slap the smugness off of Bizzell's face, but John Wayne, God rest his soul, was probably the only man who could get out of a situation in that manner.

"We'll take a look at the evidence once we can get the rest of the fire out, but I'm concerned that with those snowmobiles and four-wheelers in there too, if we can't get this contained, things are going to get a whole lot worse before they get better." Bradley turned to Diego. "You didn't answer earlier. Do you have insurance on this place?"

"Yes, we're covered in the extent of fire, and we haven't recently made any real changes." He turned back to Bizzell, and wiped at his cheek, spreading soot across his face. "What do you think, Sheriff? You think it might be Patti Lucero?"

"Now, Diego, why you want to go and open that can of worms?" the sheriff expressed his disgust with another spit of tobacco that landed close to Diego's foot. Diego frowned and kicked snow over the brown spit.

"She did make my life miserable for about a year, Sheriff, and she didn't go very far when she said she was leaving. Remember? And she's the only person I can think of who might be interested in making my life hell for any reason."

"Well, now, from what I remember, you were making her life just as miserable. What with chasing her down on the freeway and all."

Diego shook his head. Sheriff Bizzell had a history of being turned by a pretty head who was as likely to give him favors in the sack as he was by the law. He could care less what was right. He just wanted what felt good. It disgusted Diego to have to deal with such a sordid lawman. He was as close as Diego could get to justice out here, though.

"I wasn't chasing her down the freeway, sir. If you remember, she was chasing me, trying to push my truck off the road." He snorted in disgust and realized this conversation was pointless. He defended Julie again.

"I seriously doubt Julie had anything to do with this." He argued again. "Her calf was in the stall with Ginger—"

"Wait a minute. Her calf? I thought you said she was just a visitor?" Both Bizzell and Bradley were interested in that tidbit.

"It's a long story, but, regardless, she wouldn't hurt a hair on either of their heads, no matter what she thought about the ranch or me, or anything." He convinced himself this was true, but a niggling doubt welled up in the back of his brain as he spoke. Could Julie have done this? He really didn't know anything about her. But why would she? If she wasn't a gold digger, could it be that she was one of those animal rights activists? He'd made it clear that he had been in the rodeo and that his animals were used in many rodeos. He profited off of rodeos. Was she someone he couldn't trust after all? The thought scared him and made him angry. He was angry with the sheriff for making him doubt her.

"Maybe we should get her over here and have a chat with her," the sheriff drawled, shaping the snow under his feet with the toe of his pointed boot.

Diego bit his tongue as he started to defend her again, but suddenly, there she was next to him. The look on her face told Diego that she had heard it all. She stood tall and proud next to him, even though she was wearing next to nothing, topped with boots. Her face was streaked with soot and her hair was singed from a close encounter with a burning beam in the barn when she first opened Ginger's stall. But Diego thought she looked incredible. She looked like a woman about to do battle to defend her empire. He suddenly realized how much he wanted her.

She put her hand out to the fire chief first and introduced herself. She turned back to the sheriff and looked him in the eye.

"Did you want to ask me something?" Diego was proud of how she held herself when she knew she was under the gun. His doubts were somewhat assuaged by her demeanor. How could he have doubted that she would be at fault for destroying his home? Diego looked at Julie, then at the country bumpkin standing in front of him. Sheriff Bizzell had no idea how to talk to a real woman. As soon as he opened his mouth, Diego snickered inside. Julie was going to tear him apart.

***

"Well, little lady, how did you happen to be the first one to find out that this place was on fire?"

Julie blinked, but outwardly showed no sign of her surprise at his tone. Instead, she addressed the question as well as the "little lady" comment.

"My name is Julie Davenport, sir, and to answer your question, I woke up suddenly, but couldn't figure out why. I checked on the kids and thought I saw somebody running from the barn. As I went to get Diego, I smelled smoke and realized the barn was on fire. I woke Diego up so that he could start managing the fire before the fire crew could get here."

"Hmm. Seems odd you didn't wake up the people in the house with you, especially if you were in the house already?" The obvious distrust and doubt that had been cast upon Julie crushed her, but she didn't allow this to show on her face. Silently, she sucked in a breath and gathered strength from Diego. He gently rested his hand upon the small of her back and stepped a bit closer. She was bolstered by his subtle show of support. He believed her.

"I didn't wake them because I didn't want to take the

time, when I knew that Diego was closer and would know exactly what to do. I guess I thought Natalie and Gabe would first check on their kids, and I could only think about Ginger, Snowflake, Flame and the others. I didn't want the horses to suffer and I couldn't bear the idea of Diego losing them." Julie raised her shoulders and looked at the sheriff again.

"Why were you checking on the children? They aren't your children, what were you worried about?" The sheriff stared hard at Julie as he fired questions at her, not waiting for the answers.

Julie raised her head and squared her shoulders. "If you'll give me a minute to answer, I would." She glared at the sheriff, frustrated that she was in this position when all she had done was pull off the highway because her car wouldn't run.

"I was concerned that I heard something. I did not know what I heard, and the only thing I could think was that perhaps one of the kids was awake." She tucked her hands in her pockets and assumed a posture of rebellion, her shoulders still back, her elbows askew. "I had woken abruptly. I did not know what was happening exactly, and I just reacted, rather than planned."

"Why didn't you wait to hear if they actually were awake?" He scrubbed his mustache down with a beefy hand.

Julie became irritated. "Sheriff, why are you asking so many questions about me? Don't you think this is wasting our time?" Her face flushed a brilliant red as she angrily pushed her hair out of her face.

"None of this is a waste of time, lady, I have to find out what happened to this here barn." The Sheriff stared hard at Julie, noticeably eyeing her figure under the bulky jacket. Nervous and disgusted, Julie pulled her coat closed with one hand and stepped closer to Diego, who put his arm around her shoulder.

"I had nothing to do with this, sheriff, and I saw someone out here. Shouldn't we look at where she ran and see if we can find any footprints or clues or something?"

Diego nodded and Julie was relieved at his tacit agreement.

"I think we need to get out and see if we can find anything before this snow covers it up again. Julie, which way did this person go when you saw him leaving the barnyard? Wait a minute, did you say 'she'?" He turned to look straight at her. "Did you think it was a woman?"

Sheriff Bizzell interrupted, trying to take control of the situation back into his hands. "You say you saw someone. What did this person look like?" The sheriff pulled out a notepad but didn't write anything down.

"I can't tell you any details, I was up in the house, and that's pretty far away, but I just got the feeling it was a woman. The figure was small and seemed delicate, and, well, graceful."

"Men can be graceful." Bizzell huffed grumpily as she led them toward the eastern side of the barnyard. The lamp that was up on the peak of the barn cast light several feet into the night, but beyond the lamplight it was a deep dark night, and the snow was falling thickly.

"You got a flashlight?" The sheriff turned to Gabe and Diego. Gabe handed Bizell his high powered emergency light.

"Careful," Diego warned. "There's a barbed wire fence just over here. It separates the yard from the first pasture here."

"Maybe we should put this off until the morning. I can't see a thing." Sheriff Bizzell strained his eyes into the night, pursing his lips over the dip that bulged in his lower lip. Julie practically screamed in frustration. First, he was "Mr. Aggressive, Have to Solve this Crime," now he was pulling back, neglecting the investigation. It made her uneasy about his ability to find this person and bring justice to Diego, his family, and the animals.

"But we won't find footprints or anything in the morning, right?" Julie anxiously grasped Diego's sleeve. She peered up at the sky and a snowflake landed in her eye. "It's still snowing, and hasn't really let up for days." She blinked and tried to step where Diego stepped so she wouldn't keep sinking in the snow.

"Well, now, this snow is so deep, it can't fill in that fast." Again, he patronized her, his smug expression forcing her to silence.

"I don't know, Sheriff," Gabe spoke up. "It seems to me that when the wind kicks up, we'll see any prints fill up fast. Whoever it was, it was stupid to come out on a night like this. We can at least see what direction they headed in." Gabe was practical and focused, his military training kicking in where Sheriff Bizzell was failing.

"Sheriff, why don't you pull your truck closer and put your spotlight over here, and then we can see if there is anything to find tonight." Diego was practical in his logic, also frustrated with the sheriff's ineptitude.

"Well, now, that's a brilliant idea," Sheriff Bizzell drawled sarcastically, but he went and got his patrol truck from the drive and swung it around into the barnyard. He shone the spotlight on the space near the fence that Diego stood near. He got out of his vehicle and strode over to the fence.

"Do you see anything?" Julie called to the Sheriff, trying to stay back so she didn't interfere with the investigation. Not that the Sheriff seemed particularly concerned with finding anything, or with preserving the area.

"If there were footprints," Diego turned back to her, "they would be covered already, with or without wind." He rolled his eyes in the direction of the sheriff. "Look at this snow. I haven't seen it so bad in years!" He turned back to the Sheriff, who was muttering to himself. Bizzell stepped closer to the barbed wire and then knelt in the snow.

"Wait a minute, here," he paused and peered at the fence, noticing something fluttering in the breeze. "Hey, Diego, look at this." Diego stepped closer to where the sheriff knelt and whistled.

"Julie was right. Someone did come through here." A piece of black nylon was hooked on a barb on the fence.

"I told you I saw someone." Julie crossed her arms across her chest and heaved a sigh. "What is that?" Her curiosity drew her closer.

"It looks like it's a chunk of someone's jacket." The sheriff left the shred of fabric there and returned to his car for a plastic evidence bag. He removed the fabric with forceps and placed them in the bag, sealing it with his fingers. "So, now we find out who is missing a piece of their jacket." He eyeballed the black jacket that she wore that moment. "And while you aren't a suspect yet, Miss Davenport, I want to look at your jacket first."

"Of course. Fine. Shall we return to the house?" Julie's tone was accommodating but strained. Her face flushed as she realized how serious this could be. She wanted to crawl back into bed, and forget all about Edgewood and everything here. The only problem with that, she realized, was that she would never have met Diego. Slowly she realized that she was going to head home and would have to figure out how she was going to try and live without him in her life, even though she just might be so far in love with him that every waking minute would be torture without him.

"Wait a minute, Sheriff. Julie is the one who first discovered this. Why is she under suspicion?" Protectively, Diego took a step forward in front of Julie, who was suddenly warmed by his movement.

"She is wearing a black jacket, and she was the first to discover the fire. Those two things mean I need to check her story." Sheriff Bizzell moved toward his car. "You aren't standing in the way of my duty, are you Diego? This is possibly an arson investigation."

"Possibly arson." Diego turned to the barn where the firemen were packing up. "Chief Bradley thinks so too, but I think you're on the wrong track when it comes to suspects."

"I'm not so sure about that, Diego, and I don't know

why you're so quick to be without suspicion. Unless, that is, you've got something to cover up."

"Sheriff, you're grasping at straws. She told you she saw someone and you think she's telling stories. You don't even know her. I don't think that is a fair approach."

"Let's go inside where it's warm, unless, Sheriff, you need to look around more?" Julie reiterated her request to go inside. She said it because she was freezing her toes off, but also because this was quickly becoming a pissing match and she needed to reduce the tension somehow.

"Sounds like a fine idea. You lead the way."

Chapter Eighteen

Julie moved slowly, feeling real concern that she was being blamed for an action that she would never dream of committing. She watched her feet punch through the snow and reflected on the figure she had seen dart out of the barn and race off into the night. How did she know that it was a female? She had felt confident when she was telling the sheriff how it had appeared to her, but now she was beginning to doubt her judgment. Had she even seen someone? Diego seemed to believe her, but he was so gentle and kind, he wouldn't believe that anyone he had taken in would do him harm. She felt sure of that. Diego held Julie's hand as they headed toward the house. As if he knew she was thinking about him, he tugged on her hand and gazed down at her, winking at her as they neared the house. Shyly, she turned to him, her face gently softened in the dim light.

"You okay?" He asked gently.

"Yeah, he's just doing his job." She sighed, referring to Sheriff Bizzell. Her thoughts quickly shifted to her real concern. "You think Snowflake and Ginger will be okay?" Her voice shook as she thought about how close the two came to being trapped in that fire. She shivered. Diego pulled her closely to him, putting her hand in his other hand and warming them in his jacket. He slid his free arm around her.

"I think they will be fine," he assured her. "They will be okay for a few hours until it gets light, and then we can figure out what to do. I think most of them will probably have to stay out in the pasture and bed down with the cattle. They'll be okay." They stepped onto the porch and she took a deep breath.

Diego opened the door. "You okay?" He pulled her arm closer into his chest before she could step inside, and she looked up at him, dropping her head back to see him more clearly.

"Yeah," she struggled to smile and leaned into him for a moment. They stood like that until Sheriff Bizzell turned back.

"Ya'll coming? It's cold out here."

The group decided to sit by the fire in the house to examine what they knew and what they needed to know in order to understand how the barn had wound up in flames. Sheriff Bizzell stood closest to the fire, his back to the rest of them. Chief Bradley was still outside, supervising the cleanup. He would be in shortly, to offer his expert opinion about the night's events.

Sheriff Bizzell wasted no time. "Now Ms. Davenport, if you would, kindly let me see your jacket." His manners were about as polite as he was tall, but Julie didn't bother responding. She shrugged her jacket off as Diego stepped closer to help. More and more, she was grateful he was there for her to lean on.

"Sheriff, you're welcome to see this, but I was not the one who set that fire." Julie handed the jacket to him and sat on the sofa near the fire. She pulled her wet nightgown around her and shivered.

"Julie, why don't you go get changed, you're soaked." Diego leaned over her, concern evident on his face. She was soaked almost up to her hips and her lips were blue.

"No, I'm okay, I'm sure the Sheriff wants me here to answer any questions." The Sheriff was busy examining the jacket for tears or rips in the fabric.

"No, go change, little lady. It's fine. I just need this jacket." He played coy, now that he was inside. "Just don't skip town." He winked. Julie suppressed an urge to heave a giant sarcastic sigh, but she smiled slightly, glanced at Diego and went upstairs to put on some warm, and dry, clothes.

"I'll get you some coffee while you do that." Diego called after her and she nodded gratefully from the stairwell. "I'll go check what Natalie has going on in the kitchen. Sheriff, you want a cup?" Diego turned to the man as a knock came at the door. Gabe stood to let Chief Bradley in.

Julie heard the men begin to talk downstairs, but all she knew right about now was that she wanted a really hot drink, preferably with alcohol in it, and a shower. No, she decided, a shower wouldn't be such a bad idea, at all. Unfortunately, she figured, Sheriff Bizzell probably wouldn't wait for her to warm up that much. She pulled some sweats out of her tote and a second sweater that Natalie had lent to her that morning after mucking up the first when the calf was born. A ponytail and some fresh soft socks completed the ensemble and she turned around and headed back downstairs.

Chapter Nineteen

When Julie returned to the living room, it was empty save for Diego.

"Where did Sheriff Bizzell go? And didn't I hear Chief Bradley come in?" She looked around, confused.

"They didn't find much tonight." Diego ran a frustrated hand across his chin. "It's too dark to find much of anything, and even though it's still snowing, they have decided to let it be for tonight."

"And my jacket? Did he find what he was looking for?" Julie sat next to Diego on the sofa.

"Your jacket was fine. No tears. He decided you might be okay after all." Diego didn't want to concern her with the idea that the Sheriff hadn't completely ruled her out as a suspect, even though her jacket had not had any noticeable tears in it. He turned to look at her. "They are pretty confident this was no accident."

"Oh, Diego, I'm so sorry." Julie put her hand on his knee in a soft gesture of comfort.

"Thanks. I just don't know who would have done this!" He stood suddenly, agitated. He began pacing in front of the fire. "The easy answer is this girl I know, and it's especially plausible because you think you saw a woman run from the barn. But at the same time, I can't really see that happening, either." His pacing ceased momentarily and he grinned slyly. "She definitely is not athletic. You described her as graceful. I don't really see Patti as that."

He ran his hand through his hair and Julie watched, wishing it was her hand in his hair. She shivered at the thought, thinking about how soft it would be under her fingertips. "Um," She stuttered and shook her head to clear it of such sensual thoughts. "So who is this girl?"

"Here, ya'all, I have some coffee ready." Natalie bustled into the room, followed by Gabe, his hands full of more cheerful mugs of coffee. "I'm warming some stew and tortillas too." Natalie pressed a mug into Julie's hands.

"Just in the nick of time." Diego smiled down at Julie. "Natalie always has been good at using food to make things a little easier."

"Hey now, what do you mean by that?" Natalie tried

to look offended, but her grin peeked through. "Mama always had food ready when we needed it. I just think we need it often!"

Gabe looked fondly at his wife and joined in the banter. "Natalie, if you didn't feed us so well, I'd probably have blown away by now."

"We don't have to worry about that, now do we?" Diego jibed with a pointed look at Gabe's middle. Gabe was a little round, after all. Julie started to smile and gratefully sat with her coffee in the warm kitchen surrounded by warm people. She felt she'd known them all her life and loved the way they teased each other so lovingly, even in the face of a tragedy.

"How are the kids?" Julie looked at Natalie and took a sip of her coffee. Diego looked up from pouring his own, and Julie watched concern rush back into his face as he was reminded of how dangerous the fire could have become.

"Oh, they're fine. They didn't even wake up, even with the fire trucks and the commotion." Natalie smiled fondly as she thought about her children. "I think they'll be a bit surprised in the morning, though." She pulled her feet up under her on the sofa and took a sip of her coffee. "They'll be disappointed, too. Aidan especially. You know how he feels about fire trucks. And Jonas Bradley."

"Speaking of, Chief Bradley thinks this might have been arson." Diego wearily looked at the others. "Any idea who might have had the balls to do something like this?"

"You know, I've been thinking," Natalie piped up,

"What about Patti? I mean, she's the obvious culprit, but still, she never really was all that stable." Natalie glanced anxiously at Julie and bit her lip.

"Who's Patti?" Julie asked, looking around the group.

"A heartless bitch, if you want it from me," Gabe exploded.

"Now, Gabe, she was just a little off base." Diego grinned.

"Off base, my ass. She's a psycho, and it took you long enough to figure it out." Gabe drank half his mug of coffee and heaved a deep sigh. "Sorry Julie, she's just this girl that Diego dated."

"Yeah, make sure you include that past tense, Gabe. I dated her, but that was months ago. Why would she come back in and stir up trouble now?" Diego leaned back in his chair and rested his hands on his thighs.

"Because she's a loony tune?" Gabe spoke into his mug and eyeballed Julie, making her laugh with his crazy eyes.

"Okay, seriously, who is this girl?" Julie laughed, and the sound of her humor broke the tension that had been building in the room. "I mean, Diego dated her, but Gabe hated her?"

Everyone laughed at that but turned to look at Diego to field the questions.

"She was a girl that I met a year or so ago. We dated a little bit, and she thought that we were more than I did. She wanted to get married and move into the big house and run the Bed and Breakfast." He sighed. "She didn't realize that I wasn't in love with her, and she kind of went a little crazy when I broke it off with her."

"A little crazy?" Natalie stood, obviously irritated. "She keyed your truck. She broke your living room window with a brick." She ticked the offenses off on her fingers, one at a time. "She tried to run you off the bridge on the freeway. She put poison in Precious Dog's dish. You're telling me she was only a little crazy?" She grunted and turned to the fire. "If she had her way, Gabe, the kids, and me would be out on the street." She turned back to Diego, her eyes spitting sparks. "Diego, if she's only a little crazy, then you're a saint."

"But lovely sister of mine, I am a saint, remember?" Diego put his hand out and grabbed Natalie's pocket, pulling her into his arms and giving her a brotherly hug. Julie smiled at the teasing banter. She was falling in love with the whole family, that much was clear. She shook her head.

"So, is she capable of this too, then?" Julie asked, sincerely. "And if not Patti, then who else might have done something like this?"

Diego looked around and ran his hand through his hair in frustration. "I have no idea." He said quietly. "Dammit!" He exploded. "I have no idea—Gabe? What do you think?"

"Geez, Diego, beats me." Gabe went to take another gulp of coffee and realized his mug was empty. "I wish I could offer up some suggestions, but I have no idea. This town is too small to not know of anybody, in the first place, but everybody gets along with you, and with us. It just doesn't make any sense." He stood to get more coffee. "All I can think is Patti, too." He sat again and stared glumly at the fire.

"Excuse me for being nosy and getting involved in all of this, but if you broke up with her so long ago, why would she be the logical culprit now for this type of harassment?" Julie looked at Diego pointedly.

Natalie took this question though, exploding in response. "That woman is so bipolar that I wouldn't put it past her to have planned this out for months. She waited for a storm to come in, knowing that it would be difficult to manage, that clues would be hidden or buried by the weather, and that the odds of the fire department getting it under control so quickly would be slim." Natalie heaved a deep breath and sloshed coffee over the side of her mug. "She plays dumb as a box of rocks, but you give her a chance to be malicious, and she's a master. She's evil."

"The dark side is strong in that one." Gabe piped in.

"So, do you think the Sheriff is going to see things the way you do, or do you think he's decided I'm the one who has done it?" Julie looked nervously from one to another in the room.

"Honey, you didn't do it." Natalie stood and moved to comfort Julie. "I know you didn't do it. Common sense tells us you didn't do it, but beyond that, I'd like to see anyone prove that you did. I mean, really. A stranger off the street can see you don't have a harmful bone in your body, and beyond that, why would a woman set a fire to a barn then run in to save animals that were in danger?"

"No kidding. A spiteful woman who really wanted to get away would have gone back to bed and let everyone burn." Gabe put his two cents into the pot. "My money is on Patti."

"I agree with Natalie and Gabe." Diego spoke quietly from his spot on the sofa in front of the fireplace. "Don't fret, Julie. If it wasn't Patti, we'll figure it out."

Natalie stood and stretched "Well, y'all, I think I'm off to bed. Enough excitement for this lady, tonight." Natalie kissed Gabe on the forehead and nodded goodnight to Julie. She turned to Diego. "You better call Jonas tomorrow. Invite him to dinner, even, and we'll see what else we can find out about this."

Diego and Jonas had been friends for so long that dinner was a standing invitation, but in this case, Natalie was probably right. In order to find out who did this, they needed as much brain power on the case as possible. Diego's frustration was evident. He leaned back on the sofa and sighed deeply.

From across the room, Julie longed to touch him and show him how much she wanted to help make things right. She looked at his face, ragged with exhaustion and irritation. She thought about how she might smooth the worry from around his eyes and kiss away his tension, but she knew now was not the time or place, and not only that, but she wasn't sure if she was in the position to actually be able to do that anyway.

"Gabe, tomorrow we're going to have to figure something out for those horses."

"I already thought about that. We'll put the goats in with Ginger. They'll herd together a bit until we can get something fixed up. I already called John and Frank and let them know." Gabe poked at the fire, moving a log so that a cloud of embers rose in the heat. "They were fit to be tied and were headed out here, but I let them know that everything was okay, so I think I convinced them to stay in. They'll be here early in the morning."

Diego snickered. "Yeah, if I know those guys, they'll be here in an hour anyway. They won't stay away until morning."

As if on cue, a knock sounded on the door. Diego smiled. "See what I mean?"

He opened the door to admit two rugged looking men in identical brown canvas jackets and worn denim jeans.

"Hey there, Frank!" Diego slapped the older man on the shoulder and stepped aside to allow space for the two men to enter. "I knew it wouldn't be long before you showed up."

"We saw the flames just before Gabe called, but we had to plow the side road to get here. Sorry it took us so long."

"We got it under control." Diego rubbed the back of his neck and walked to the fireplace. "Fortunately the fire department got here fast. We only lost part of the barn, and all of the livestock were safe. Some of the equipment is probably ruined, but that can't be helped."

"Would the two of you like some coffee?" Julie stood and stepped toward the kitchen.

"Yes, ma'am," John replied. "I'd love a cup. Dad?" John looked at his father who nodded also. If Frank hadn't gray hair that peeked out in his sideburns, the two could have been twins. Symmetrical grins flashed at her from across the room, both out of sun-lined, but handsome faces. Both wore black cowboy hats tilted at opposite angles. Julie felt as if she had just stepped into an old western movie, looking at the two of them.

"Oh, hey John, Frank, this is Julie. She's staying with us for a few days. She was the one who first spotted the fire." Diego made the introductions as the men nodded in her direction.

Julie slid seamlessly into the role of hostess, and it surprised even her, especially after such a traumatic night. She was a natural at making people feel comfortable, even when she was stressed to her nails, and she'd always felt more in control when others seemed out of it. She wondered if she owed that to Adam. She shook her head and then speared Diego with a dazzling smile. She watched him blink dazedly as he realized that Frank was asking him a question, then stepped into the kitchen for more coffee.

"What did the sheriff have to say about this?"

"He thinks someone set the fire, and for once, I think he might actually be right. We just have no idea who would want to, or who actually would do such a thing."

Gabe looked at Diego and carefully stepped into the conversation. "Sheriff Bizzell thinks Julie might have had something to do with it."

"But she didn't!" Diego's vehemence had all three men looking at him under their eyebrows. "She didn't. I mean, why would she?" He stared into the fire as the men rustled behind him. Julie stepped back into the room at that moment.

"The good sheriff thinks I did it because I'm odd woman out here." She set down two cups of coffee and handed the third to Diego, looking straight into his eyes. "I didn't set that fire, but I can understand why he might question that I would. I mean, I am a perfect stranger, after all."

"But why show up suddenly here, now, and then start a fire?" Gabe looked straight at her. "It doesn't make sense. It's too perfect. Something else is going on." Julie acknowledged his quiet show of support with a nod.

"Well, we'll just have to figure it out, and I'll stick around at least until you guys know I had nothing to do with this." She looked at Diego again, whose gaze was making her warmer than the blaze of the fire in the grate against the back of her legs.

"At least you'll be sticking around." John and Frank looked at each other at that. Guarded astonishment crossed both of their faces. Diego was not one to vocally approve of a woman in front of others. In fact, he wasn't one to be so distracted, period.

Frank tucked his hands in his pockets and leaned against the mantel. "What about that new feller who moved in on the old widow's place? Wasn't he asking about some of your property?"

"Jarrett Smith?" Diego looked up at the older man with new interest. "You think he might have something to do with this?"

"He did come around the other day asking if you were interested in selling the back forty acres. I think he was interested in more than just the acreage, too. He was eyeballing some of the cattle too." John tucked his hands in his pockets too, characteristic of his father.

Julie watched the two men, thinking about how similar they appeared, even though she had just met them.

"Well, who is this guy?" Julie interjected, interested in any lead that might clear any suspicion about her involvement. Somehow she had a feeling that Sheriff Bizzell wasn't going to just drop her as a suspect just because her jacket wasn't torn. He seemed like the kind of guy who wanted an easy answer, instead of the right answer. He seemed a lot like Adam, actually. She'd had enough experience with Adam to know what that looked and felt like.

"Jarrett Smith is new around here," Diego replied. "He moved into an old property about a mile away, and he's been checking things out around here. Evidently he wants to run a couple hundred head of cattle, but the widow's place won't field that many."

"But your property will." John was putting sugar into his coffee as he spoke. He raised his mug to Julie. "Fine coffee, thanks for that." Julie smiled in response.

"So, if he wants your property, why would he do something to destroy it?" Julie felt out of place, but concerned, so she felt it was her right to interject her opinion. "Doesn't that almost seem too easy, too? Some guy shows up out of the blue and then your barn burns down? Why not your house, instead?" She stood and started to pace. "If you get rid of the house, then there is no place to live, easier to give up, right?" She paused for a breath and the men looked at each other.

"You've got a good point." Diego stood as well. "Ah, hell. I have no idea what to think right now. And I'm about beat. Let's hash this out tomorrow morning." He turned to Frank and John. "First thing tomorrow, we need to set a shelter set up for Ginger and the new calf. We'll put Flame out to pasture with the others and they can shelter out with the cattle."

The men nodded, now that a game plan was in place. They zipped their coats and headed for the door.

"We'll see you early. I think we might also have to pay a visit to our new neighbor." Gabe followed the men to the door and let them out into the night.

"Diego, do you really think there might be someone who wants to destroy your barn to get you off this property?"

"We'll find out, I guess!" Diego's stress strained his voice, but he tucked a strand of hair behind her ear. "Don't worry any more tonight. Just head for bed and I'll see you at breakfast." He smiled tenderly and she grasped his hand.

"I just feel terrible that all of this is happening." She fretted, fidgeting with his fingers. Diego grinned.

"Julie, go to bed. Things will make more sense tomorrow." He kissed her on the forehead and forcibly turned her toward the stairs, almost pushing her in the direction of her bedroom. "Goodnight, beautiful."

Julie turned once to look over her shoulder as she headed up the stairs. Diego was lost in thought, staring into the flames. Abruptly, he banked the fire and headed out the door toward his own place in back.

Chapter Twenty

Diego gazed out the picture window that, in the daytime, showed the splendor of the snow covered mountains behind his modest casita. Tonight the view was merely darkness, but it sparkled with the continually falling snow. This "mother-in-law quarters" helped enclose the patio of the main house and was perfect for a bachelor. He had helped design the small space, believing that efficiency led to comfort for a single man. Diego loved the main house, but without his mother there, it had always seemed off somehow. She had made the place alive. He loved having the kids in there, they brightened every social hour in the big house, but he loved the peace and quiet of his little place.

Diego reflected on Julie and how small she seemed, but how she was able to liven up a room with just a smile.

"She's just passing through." He sighed, trying to remind himself that Julie wasn't staying. It didn't work. He smiled as he thought about her reaction to ol' Pete this morning. That seemed like a million years ago. The day had given them an opportunity to grow close, and tonight's fire in the barn had shown him her extent of character. He respected this woman more with every passing moment.

He lit a small fire in the fireplace designed to warm both the living room and his bedroom, with the view of the flames from both sides. The high ceilings made the place feel extraordinarily spacious, though he could step into each room with very little effort. As late as it was, and even as exhausted as he felt, he didn't think he'd be falling back to sleep any time soon. He stripped his shirt and tossed it over the recliner. He unbuttoned his pants and kicked off his boots. Distracted and half undressed, he sat in front of the fire and rested his hand on his chin.

The idea that perhaps his new neighbor might have something to do with the fire was bothering him, eating at his gut. He hadn't met the man, didn't know him from Joseph, but he knew Jarrett Smith had been over to Frank and John's and had introduced himself. The men's loyalty was deep and sincere, and they had made it clear that Diego wasn't in the market to sell any of his land, no matter what the price offered.

Both Frank and John had mentioned how smooth Jarrett appeared on the surface, but he seemed too smooth—almost oily. That had set them off from the stranger pretty quickly. Frank and John were not altogether reliable when it came to newcomers though. Both had pretty severe trust issues on that end. Diego needed to get out tomorrow and meet this man.

His thoughts tripped from Jarrett Smith and the damaged barn to the look on Julie's face when the sheriff had practically accused her of setting the fire. He smiled at her frustration and the way she had put that backwoods know-it-all in his place. Somehow, Diego knew she had not been the one to cause the destruction. He'd seen the way Julie responded to both Ginger and Snowflake and knew without a hesitation that she would not put those animals in harm's way. He wanted to believe she also felt something for him. Something like what he was feeling for her, and that feeling made him believe she would never destroy his livelihood with a reckless fire.

A bold knock sounded at the door and his heart jumped. Perhaps Julie was coming to visit him. He ran a hand through his hair and pulled open the door.

"Hey, stranger!" It definitely was not Julie. Patti, the woman he desperately wished he had left alone a year ago when he'd met her at the tri-county arena, stood on his doorstep instead. She held up a bottle of wine that might have set her back three bucks and smiled over-brightly up into his face, her rouged lips garish in the darkness of the porch shadows. Briefly, he wondered again what had possessed him to introduce himself to her. It had to have been the third shot of Jack Daniels that he had tossed back the night he'd gotten trampled by the biggest, meanest bull he'd ever come across, Blues Traveler.

"Patti." He reached for the shirt that he'd tossed on the back of the recliner as he'd come in an hour before. "What are you doing here?"

"Awww, don't put that back on." Patti purred as she slid around the door and into Diego's space. She stroked a hand over Diego's broad chest as he struggled into the shirt. Snow blew in behind her, and she slyly closed the door with her foot as she wrapped her other arm around him. The bottle of wine dangled over his shoulder, and she slid closer, her breasts brushing his bare skin through the open shirt.

Diego caught her hand and opened the door she had just shut.

"You need to go, Patti."

"Come on, Diego," she cooed, "don't turn an old friend out into this cold night. I just wanted to come visit and see how you were doing." Patti pulled her arm free and moved over to sit in his armchair as she continued to flirt with her eyes. Irritated, Diego kicked the door shut with his foot and turned to face the big breasted but small brained woman who had needled her way into his living room.

"In the middle of the night?" He felt like tearing his hair out. "Patti, it's late, it's been a hard day, and I have no idea why you are here. Don't you remember how it ended for us? Why are you here?" Diego sighed in frustration, thinking he never had understood women anyway. He pulled his shirt closed and considered adding his jacket as a hint, but he knew she'd never take it.

"I missed you." Patti shaped her lips into a pout. "I've never known anyone like you, Diego, and I want to try again with you!"

Diego snorted. "Some timing. It's been over a year since we ended things, remember? And, not only that, but it's the middle of the night, and snowing like the devil out there." If he'd thought she was crazy before, he was justified in thinking that now. She hardly had a jacket on over her thin sweater in this kind of weather. Instantly, an image of Julie in her heavy parka lying in the snow the night before popped into his mind. He sent up a quick prayer, thankful that he had been there to help her. He wished again the woman in front of him was Julie, and not this trollop.

Patti stood again, running her hand up and down his arm. She pushed her hips toward him and flung her arms around his neck. "Diego, I just had the feeling I needed to be here right now. I didn't care that it was snowing. I love you, Diego, don't you know that?" Diego took her hands from around his neck and pushed her gently away.

"Patti, you need to go. It's over. It's been over. You

know as well as I do that it didn't work out once, it won't again." He finished buttoning his shirt and opened the door again, gesturing at Patti to leave.

"But Diego, it was so much fun, don't you remember?"

"I remember you trying to drive me off the freeway in weather similar to this." He glared at her and crossed his arms in front of his chest. He glanced meaningfully at the open door, but she wasn't taking the hint.

"I don't want to go Diego," she cooed again. "And besides, don't you want to know what happened to your barn?"

Slowly Diego shut the door and turned to face Patti, his face carefully blank.

"What do you know about the barn?" He stepped softly into the room, afraid that any sudden move might make her stop talking. Fury rose in his throat as he imagined what role she had in the devastation that had hit his ranch. "Did you do it?" He advanced to stand in front of her.

She coyly dipped her face and gazed up at him through her eyelashes. "Oh, I didn't set your barn on fire. But I might know who did." Now she was playing games with him. He wanted to wrap his hands around her neck and strangle the truth out of her, but he knew that wouldn't get him anywhere other than jail. Diego had been taught to treat women with respect, even if this one hadn't really earned much. His fingers itched to teach her a lesson, though. If he pulled her over his knee for a spanking, she'd enjoy that too much.

"Patti, do you know who damaged my place, or why

they would want to?"

"I might know something," she hedged. She tucked her hands in her tiny pockets, subtly tugging her jeans a bit lower on her hips. Diego was not distracted. He'd had a taste of her charms before and he was unimpressed. She didn't offer much beyond a quick roll in the hay, and he was definitely seeking more for his life. Right now, all he could think about was who would want to destroy his barn, and potentially, some of his livestock, and most likely, his livelihood.

Chapter Twenty One

Julie sat in her room staring at the wall. Part of her was struggling with who would set Diego's barn on fire, and part of her was worried about Adam's persistence. His phone calls were becoming more random and odd, and she'd had another message from him waiting on her phone when she had gotten back to her room after meeting Frank and John. She was tired. It was the middle of the night, and in little over a day, she had witnessed a miracle birth, basically been accused of arson, was stranded in a foreign town, sleeping in someone else's bed, and her head was spinning. Enough was enough. She wanted to cry, but she didn't have the energy. She thought about going out to Diego's apartment to sit with him, but worried that it was too late. She peered out the window and saw his lights were still on. Perhaps he wanted her to visit too. Without another thought, she grabbed her coat, slipped on her boots and left the house, following the sidewalk to Diego's place.

Julie knocked on the door before she heard the female voice. Once she did, she turned to go, but as she took her first step off the porch, the door was wrenched open, and a disheveled and obviously irritated Diego peered out into the night.

"I'm sorry to bother you," she stammered, but he grabbed her hand and pulled her into the room. Julie stumbled and Diego caught her, apologizing into her hair. He stood next to her as she regained her balance, her hand still in his, a glare on his face.

"You didn't bother me," he grumbled. "She did," he said with an irritated swipe of his arm in the direction of a woman with the largest and most undressed breasts Julie had ever seen. The red sweater dipped dangerously low on the pair of girls that stood at attention. Julie barely saw the woman's face, she was so astounded at the twin mounds before her. That was a testament to God's glory, she thought briefly, before she turned back to Diego and took in the unbuttoned shirt and the jeans that hung low on his hips, the zipper barely holding them in place.

"Uh, I think I probably did bother you. I'm really sorry to barge in here. I'll get out of your hair." She disentangled her hand from his larger one and took a step toward the door.

"Diego, who is this?" The woman pouted and put a hand on her hip. Her long fingernails were lacquered with the shiniest, reddest nail polish Julie had ever seen, and she suddenly wished she didn't keep her fingernails in a square blunt with the natural color. She would have given anything for long nails at that moment, just so she had something to chew on. Or to scratch with.

Diego dropped into his armchair facing the fire, his head in his hands. "Look, I'm tired, frustrated, angry, and a little disappointed here. Julie, don't go. Patti, you need to explain yourself, and it's really none of your business who she is."

"Oh really." Patti let that phrase drip off her tongue as innocently as she could, but to Julie, it was a challenge. Julie smiled sweetly and nodded, immediately understanding what was going on. She realized her mistake in thinking this woman was any threat when it came to Diego. She let her hand drop gently to his shoulder blade. Comfortingly, she placed her hand on his shoulder and focused her eyes on Patti.

"And why are you here?" Julie asked with a catlike smile as she felt, rather than saw Diego turn his head to gaze into her face. A dimple danced at the corner of her mouth.

"I saw the fire, and I know who set it."

"Oh really? You have information to prove this is arson?" Julie squared up against the woman standing at the stereo, changing CD's as if she lived in Diego's apartment. Julie felt like she was going to become violent for the first time in her life. She was seething as she watched this woman pretend she belonged there. She cocked her head at Patti. "Why didn't you report that to the sheriff? They were out here for over an hour earlier. If you saw something, you should have reported it then." She turned to Diego. "And do you believe whatever it was that she said?"

"What she says makes sense, since we did find some evidence that the fire was set, but I agree that it's pretty convenient that you show up here right after the fire, Patti. And that you didn't report anything to Sheriff Bizzell." He turned on her too, then walked over and took the CD's out of her hand. "Why is that?"

"Diego," she crooned, "I was scared! It was a big fire and everybody was in such a panic. I didn't know who to talk to first."

Diego scoffed. "That's ridiculous. When a crime is committed, especially out here, don't you think you should let people know what you saw?"

Patti's lips pursed and heaved a petty sigh.

"You know what, Patti, I've asked you to go, I think it's past time for you to head home." Diego had reached the limits of his patience.

"But Diego, I risked my life getting here in this weather. Are you really going to turn me out?"

Brazenly, she slid her hand up his chest again, her eyes narrowing as she glanced in Julie's direction.

"Yes, I really am going to turn you out. In fact, I'm kicking you out. You need to call Sheriff Bizzell, and I am going to also. If you saw something, you better spill it. I want to know what happened here, and I want to know who did it."

Patti turned with a pout, but Julie was already at the door, shepherding her out. "Time to go!"

"Diego," Patti started, but Julie interrupted, trying to be diplomatic, but fed up with the woman who stood before her, still trying to assert her place in Diego's life. Julie wasn't going to give Patti an inch.

"Patti, thank you for sharing what you know with us. Now, I think you should go," Julie looked at the clock over the mantel. "It's already four in the morning, and we have a lot to manage tomorrow with this fire and beginning a new barn." Julie smiled, though she felt her lips might fall off for the effort and her irritation. "We'll probably talk more with you tomorrow. I imagine we'll all be meeting with Sheriff Bizzell." She turned to Diego. "Don't you think, honey?"

Patti turned to Julie, her face transformed into a mask of anger, but Julie barely saw it, because the grin Diego shot at her blinded her. Her heart began to race and she smiled back, both of them forgetting Patti for the moment. They stepped closer to one another and Patti stomped to the door.

"Fine. I'll leave, but Diego, you'll regret this. You think this bitch is going to make you happy?" She spat the words at Diego, but his eyes were glued to the blonde haired beauty who had bewitched him from the moment he first saw her the day before.

Belatedly, he turned back to Patti and smiled gently. "She already does." He draped his arm around Julie and beamed at Patti. "Night, Patti."

Patti slammed the door shut behind her and Diego wrapped his arms around Julie's shoulders. "Thank you," he mumbled, as he rested his chin on her head. Julie's arms tightened around his waist and she grinned.

"You seriously dated that girl?" She stepped back and cheekily winked at Diego. "Whatever possessed you?" She shook her head in teasing disbelief.

"There aren't many options out here," he grinned in response.

"Evidently," she answered. "She does have some pretty glorious assets," she arched an eyebrow as she continued teasing Diego. He just shook his head, the same silly grin on his face.

"Too much, is what she has." He rolled his eyes.

Julie giggled at his response. "I never would have pegged you to date a woman who had more going for her in the physical department than in the brain department." She jibed, still a little shaken by his blinding grin. As much as she teased, her insides were coming unraveled at being so close to him, his scent mingled with the hint of smoke that emanated from the shirt he'd worn earlier.

"I know, I know, she came along in a moment of weakness." He paused, reflective. "Someday, I really would like to get married." Grinning again, he said, "For about a day, I thought she might be a candidate for that, but she really was not what I was looking for." He stepped back and took Julie's hand, leading her to the sofa in front of the fire. He settled her, stoked the fire and leaned back next to her. "When I first met Patti, she was interesting, and interested in what I had going on. I didn't realize she was just looking for a way out of her life." He draped his arm over Julie's shoulders again, resting his hand on her hip. Julie snuggled in, tucking her feet under her on the sofa. She sighed contentedly.

"Well, you seem like you have a lot going for you, I guess she just saw the good stuff in you, too."

"What she saw was a lot of acreage, a beautiful old house that she coveted, and a bunch of livestock that she knew would feed her. She's not my type. I want a partner, not someone I have to constantly take care of and cater to." He scrubbed his hand over his face in frustration. "I guess I kind of knew it when I met her, but really, I was blind to a lot of her flaws at first because I was lonely and wanted a woman in my home."

Julie added, "And she is really pretty, on top of that."

"Yeah, she's pretty." He agreed and the dimple by his eye jumped. "Pretty ugly." He winked and sighed. "She really has some major issues. I should have seen it before I got mixed up with her, but..." He let the sentence trail off as he tucked a strand of hair away from Julie's face with his free hand. "I guess I just knew there was always something more out there. I was just waiting to see what it looked like." He gazed into Julie's blue eyes and once more, was reminded of rolling plains and shifting grasses. Her eyes were so lovely to just look at. In the firelight, they twinkled with good humor and kindness, but he could see the fatigue beginning to take its toll on her.

He leaned back a bit to get a better look at her, though her face was tilted up toward his. She sighed and grinned weakly at him, her eyes drifting closed as he watched. He watched her tenderly as she lost the battle with her eyelashes and a weak snore escaped her mouth. He gently pulled the afghan down over her hips. She settled in further.

"I could get used to this," he whispered softly, briefly tightening his hand around the woman who was becoming more and more precious to him by the second.

"Um-hmm," she sighed, more asleep than awake and Diego too closed his eyes, contented for the moment with the idea that even though his barn lay smoldering, his life was, after all, piecing itself together nicely.

Chapter Twenty Two

When Julie woke, she started to stretch, the peace of sleep peeling off slowly. Then she felt Diego move beside her. Momentarily confused, she tensed, noting her surroundings. The fire had gone down, only embers smoldering in the fireplace. She was in Diego's bed, his warm body wrapped around hers. Somehow he had carried her to bed last night, but she didn't remember it. The heavy quilt that covered the two of them was draped over most of his body, but his shoulders were bare and broad. She noticed the dark curls that gently covered his chest and she smiled softly. She almost ran her hand through a whorl that curled just at the cleft of his collarbones under his chin, but instead, she just watched him sleep. She loved the rhythm of his gentle breathing, the way his lips begged to be kissed, the lashes that floated on his cheeks. She felt like she could watch him sleep all day.

"Whatcha lookin' at?" He mumbled sleepily and tightened around her, pulling her back to rest against his chest.

Julie smiled and rested her head gently on his shoulder. "Just lookin'."

Suddenly she realized she was in his bed, and that she hadn't stayed in her room at the Bed and Breakfast. She bolted upright, looking down to see where her clothes were. She sighed half in relief, half in disappointment, because all were still on her. Diego still had his jeans on, but had stripped the shirt again, evidently. That meant there had been no excitement once they hit the sheets. She was glad of it, because she sure couldn't remember it, anyway. That would have been a shame.

She flipped the quilt back and started to get out of bed, but paused and turned to look back at Diego. He was watching her through slitted eyes, the blues dark as midnight under the smoky lashes. She smiled and he grinned, suddenly even more catlike.

"I probably should go…" she hesitated, shyly looking at him from under her own lashes. She really hoped he would ask her to stay, but she was profoundly aware of the impropriety of the moment.

"Why?" he reached for her lazily, and she went easily.

"Natalie and Gabe…" she whispered, her eyes closing slightly as she swayed toward him.

Diego laughed and pulled Julie to him, his hands under her hips. He began to nibble at her neck, teasing her sweater down with his chin. "Natalie and Gabe won't mind, I promise."

Julie moaned contentedly, surprised at the noises that escaped her. "Why do you do this?" Julie protested weakly, trying to think of one good excuse for not going with the feelings that were crowding out any sort of good judgment she might have once had.

Diego murmured, "Why do I do what?" He nuzzled his nose along her hairline and his hands slipped under the back of her shirt.

"Make me feel like this."

"How do you feel?

"Like I'm melting." She put her hand on the back of his head and pulled him closer to kiss him even deeper. Shocks ran through Diego as he closed his eyes, feeling her tongue caress his softly.

"I feel it too, honey," he whispered against her lips.

He rolled over on top of her to deepen the kiss, and

144

she moaned again, feeling him press into her hip. Diego slid his hand down her side, pushing his hand under her sweater and cupping a breast. Julie sighed, her defenses breached. She pushed her hips toward him, her arms pulling him closer. She felt like exploding, her desire was so great.

"Diego," she gasped his name between ragged breaths. "I'm not prepared for this." She whispered, her common sense fighting to exert itself, but his body on top of hers had Julie spinning out of control. She felt his weight, smelled his scent, breathed in his kiss, and half of her begged the other half to give it control.

"I have something," he whispered in return.

"That's not what I mean."

"You mesmerize me." He pulled up on his elbow and played with the hair splayed across his pillow. He pulled back, clearly reluctant to scare her off. "Honey, if you don't want to do this, I won't push you." Her eyes shifted from his face to his chest to the ceiling, as she tried to resist the desire that was about to consume her.

"I want to, but it just seems too fast," Julie was struggling to come up with excuses. The blood in her head pounded for release with Diego's connection, and she was confused to still have her clothing on.

"It is fast. It's right, though. I can feel it."

"You have protection?"

"I can take care of that, but I won't do anything you don't want," Diego's concern for her well-being pushed a giggle to Julie's lips. "If you aren't ready..."

"Diego, I admit I'm afraid." Julie whispered softly,

tears welling in the corner of her eyes.

"There is nothing to be frightened of. If you want this, I want this."

She responded with a decision. She began kissing the gentle cleft of his chin, scratching her lips on the hairs that started coming in overnight. She kissed his chin and his cheek and pulled his head down to kiss his lips once more. He sighed into her and gathered her in his arms, pulling her tightly to him. She molded her body to fit his and suddenly he rolled off.

"Diego? What's the matter?"

"I want this, Julie, you are just so beautiful, so incredible," He sat up on the side of the bed, his hands between his legs, his head hung down. "I just don't want to make mistakes with you, Julie. Already, you mean so much to me." Sheepishly, he grinned over his shoulder at her. "Do you know what I mean? I just don't want to ruin it."

Julie smiled and sat up, sliding her arms around his bare waist. "We're both adults, Diego. We can do these things. Remember?" She grinned wickedly and pulled back to pull her sweater off. Her breasts shone whitely in the light, the nipples pinkened and aroused. Diego sucked in a breath at the sight. Julie took his hand and gently placed it on her breast. "I am afraid. But I want this. I want you, Diego."

"Are you sure this is what you want?" His arm slid around her waist again and he lowered his head to kiss her lips. She moaned and he kissed her neck then moved his lips to her breast, warming it with his breath in the chilled early morning air.

"This is definitely what I want," she sighed. Her decision made, she was ready to throw caution to the wind and make it happen. She hoped her sigh told him all he needed to know, that they could stop talking, that they could start loving. It worked.

Together, they laid back on the sheets, his body above hers.

Chapter Twenty Three

Natalie turned on the oven and began to prepare the

eggs and ham and other ingredients for a baked casserole. Nobody seemed to be moving too quickly today, after the events of the evening before, and she was calmly watching her brother out of the corner of her eye as she worked on feeding the multitudes. Diego stood next to her, his hip on the counter, his mind stuck on Julie's satisfied smile from this morning. The woman of his dreams sat delicately across the room, her concentration on the cookbook that Natalie had left on the table, a hint of a smile tinged the corners of her mouth. Every so often, Diego would catch her glancing at him, and her smile would grow, threatening to knock the air out of his lungs each time. He couldn't take his eyes off her.

He must have done something right to deserve that glorious vision.

Natalie turned on the faucet and began to fill the sink with dishes to wash. "You did the deed, didn't you?" Natalie murmured. "The two of you are positively glowing." Her sly grin snaked across her face and she nudged Diego with her elbow. "You're a dog, dude."

Diego flushed, but his answer was muffled by an avalanche of kids and calf as they exploded into the kitchen. The calf scrambled to make purchase on the shiny linoleum, his hooves clicking delicately as he barreled headlong into Diego. One by one, kids clamped onto Natalie's hips and beaming faces looked up into hers as they began to beg.

"It smells good in here!

"Yeah, like apple pie!"

"Is it ready?"

"Can we have some?"

"Do you have hot chocolate, too?"

Gracefully and happily, Natalie turned to each child, smiling into their eyes and responding patiently to their request. She casually touched each one, gently demonstrating maternal affection.

Diego smiled at the familiar ruckus the kids made and he watched his sister love her kids from within her soul. His heart warmed at the idea that someday, maybe he could have the same thing. His mind turned to Julie and how she seemed to fill his heart, his bed, and suddenly his life. She did more than fill his life; she was larger than his life. He could smell her scent in his nose, hear her moans in the back of his mind. Distractedly, he poured water from the sink into a pitcher.

"So you did, huh?" Natalie grinned at her big brother, while disengaging one child after another from her hip. Julie herded the kids back out of the room, whirlwinds leaving energy sprinkled across the floor and in the air. Diego turned to Natalie, the expression on his face one that she'd never seen. Playfully, she clutched her chest. "Did my big brother go and fall in love?" She sat heavily in the chair at the table, hand still covering her heart. "I never thought I'd live to see the day!" Eyes candidly open in wonder and a little bit of sarcastic humor, she watched Diego try to figure out what he was doing with a pitcher of water in his hand.

"I think I did, Nat." He dumped the pitcher back in the sink, grabbed a towel and sat heavily across from her as well. "She's amazing. I never dreamed I'd meet someone like her."

"Yeah, but what are you going to do now? Isn't she planning to leave when her car is ready?" Natalie rearranged the placemat, then stood to put some water on for tea. Her eyes no longer held humor, but now a sisterly concern.

"Yes, she's planning to, but I'm hoping to talk her into staying." He fiddled with the towel. "You don't think I'm rushing things, do you?"

"Well, yeah, you've only known her a couple of days, but think about our history." She adjusted the heat under the tea kettle and spoke over her shoulder. "Isn't it kind of interesting that you'd fall in love so quickly? It's kind of like mom and dad, isn't it?" She knew he understood the story of how his parents had met and a week later, eloped. They'd never left the other's side until the day they died.

He grinned again. "Yeah, it is. I think she feels the same for me, but..." His voice trailed off. "I have to find out if she's willing to stay."

"Well, maybe she just needs the right motivation. Tomorrow's Christmas Eve. Why don't you remind her of that, and tell her she's welcome to stay." Natalie grabbed a new coffee mug out of the cupboard and slid a teabag out of its wrapper. "Just remind her that there won't be any stores or gas stations open, and besides, the kids are counting on her to be there. They've already put together a gift for her."

"How do you think she'll take that?" Diego looked up at her quizzically. "Hey, do you have any of that pumpkin loaf left?"

Natalie pulled out the leftover sweet, and cut a slice as she thought about the emotions she saw reflected in his eyes. She was concerned that Julie would break his heart, but she also was amused that he was finally opening his mind and heart to the possibility that there was someone out there for him. Patti had definitely not been the right choice as a lover.

"She'll feel guilty because she didn't do any gifts for them, but she'll get over it." Natalie licked her fingers as she pushed the plate with his slice over to him. "I like her, Diego. She's quiet, she's kind, she's concerned. And how many people are willing to risk their life to save someone else's livestock?" She eyeballed the rest of the pumpkin loaf. "Man, that really is good."

Diego reached over to the dish drainer and grabbed a fork. He handed it to her and took another bite of his own.

"So what are you going to do?" She asked over a mouthful of cake. "I think you push the issue. I mean," she swallowed and cut another forkful. "It's not like you're going to run into her on the street next week, if you just let her go."

"You're right. Speaking of, Patti showed up last night after the fire. Julie came over and it turned into a pretty awful introduction."

Natalie choked on her pumpkin loaf and Diego pounded her back.

"Patti showed up at your place? In the middle of the night?" Her momentary fit began to subside and she took a swig of Diego's coffee. "Yuck, what the heck have you put in this?"

"Just coffee, sis, you know I like it black."

"Doll it up with some sugar, at least." She stood and fixed up her tea. "Well, tell me how it went between the two of them. That can't have been cool. And what was she doing there in the middle of the night?"

"Patti? Or Julie?"

"Duh, Diego. Patti. What was that bitch doing? Gloating over the fire?"

"She insists she had nothing to do with it. Julie came over pretty soon after Patti got there and you should have seen her feathers ruffle. She did not like the idea of another woman in my place, that was evident." He half snickered at the memory. "She's a firecat, that Julie."

"Oh, I can see that. She definitely has the makings of an incredible Garcia, that's for sure."

Diego flushed. "Slow down, Nat. She's probably leaving."

"Not if you ask her nicely, Diego. She's got it as badly for you, as you obviously have it for her. Go get her. Show her how wonderful you are." Natalie sipped her tea and grimaced. "Too hot."

"That's for sure."

"I meant my tea, weirdo."

He stood and headed for the door. "Wish me luck, sis."

"Good luck!" She called after him, still amused that he was suddenly in a lovely little mess of his own.

Chapter Twenty Four

The living room fireplace was roaring with a hot fire and Julie stood before it, musing over the night's events. She knew her skin was glowing after Diego's lovemaking because her entire body was still vibrating from the thorough loving. Even showering and dressing couldn't erase the sensations of his hands on her skin, and she grinned when her mind so easily conjured up how perfectly her body fit under his. She could easily slide right back under his sheets right now, but since the entire household was up and Frank and John were expected any moment, she knew she should probably get her head back together. Sheriff Bizzell had seemingly let her off the hook, according to Diego, but Julie didn't believe it for a minute. She had the feeling he was going to put her under the microscope again today.

"Speak of the devil." Julie's heart leapt as she noticed Diego in the doorway. "I was just thinking about you." She gazed under her eyelashes at the man before her. His eyes smoldered and she realized he was feeling the same thing she was. If there weren't other things more important, she imagined they could easily spend the rest of the day in his bed doing amazing things to one another.

"You were, huh?" Magnetized, the two stepped toward each other, but at that moment, a brief knock sounded and the door opened. In strolled John, stamping snow off his boots.

"Hey Diego, I was hoping you were still in here."

"John, how're the roads?"

"The wind has started to kick it up in drifts, so we'll have to plow a few times, I'm thinking. Dad's still out there in the driveway trying to clear it out with the plow." John removed his hat and held it in his hands. "It's colder than a witch's tit out there," he nodded at Julie, "'scuse me, ma'am."

Julie grinned and stepped to the side of the hearth. "Come warm up over here."

John stamped his boots one more time to remove the rest of the packed snow from the tread and moved over by the hearth, a grin on his face too.

"Is it still snowing?" She noticed the snowflakes on his shoulders, and looked between him and Diego, dumbfounded. "Are you serious? How long is this snow supposed to last?"

"It's not snowing heavily now, I think it's on the tail-end." John sniffed the cold out of his nose. "Hey, what's Nat got cooking? It smells amazing in here."

"She's got some late breakfast brewing. You and your dad want to eat and then we'll get to some work?"

"Nah, we actually ate awhile ago. We also cleared that cow out."

"That was a good idea. It's a pity she died, but we'll have to think about how we're breeding these females—we probably shouldn't trust Pete out there with them. He might need to be penned up when winter's coming."

"I think that's a pretty good idea." Julie listened to the two men strategize for a better winter next year and she daydreamed about being able to stay. Diego looked so good to her from every angle. And she loved

154

the idea of the freedom of the ranch. She wanted to learn everything about living with the livestock and living off the land. And she enjoyed the sense of family that was so rich in this house.

"With the wind kicking up, we're not out of the woods, yet, though. I'm just glad that if a fire had to happen, it happened before the winds could carry it to this house." Diego opened the closet and reached for his canvas jacket and gloves.

"Are you heading outside?" Julie asked and moved toward the door.

"I better go survey the damage with John, and get Frank out of that snowplow or we won't hear the end of it from him." Diego and John exchanged grins. "He loves to plow, but he loves to complain more."

"You know he's all bluff. He just likes the attention." John winked at Julie as he pulled the door open to leave. "He's just a big ol' softy under all his grizzly exterior."

"Natalie's in the kitchen, unless you want to come out here with us." Diego zipped his coat and stepped closer to the door. "After we get some stuff done here, we'll go check on your car, okay?"

Dread suffused her soul at the idea of leaving this guy. She smiled to cover what was happening in her mind and asked, "You'll need some lunch, right?" Julie wasn't quite ready to relinquish the gaze she'd gotten a moment before from Diego, but she knew he had work to do. "I'll go help Natalie get something around for when you return."

Diego put his Stetson on and followed John out the

door, leaning back inside to peck a quick kiss on her cheek. "See you in a minute, gorgeous."

Giddily, Julie closed the door behind him, a grin from ear to ear. "Oh Lord." In the blink of an eye, she went from sheer misery to outright euphoria. She put her hand to her heart and shook her head. She might have to leave him in a day or two, but for today, he was consuming her heart and soul and it was welcome. She almost danced a jig, but at that moment a calf came barreling out of somewhere and knocked into her, a gaggle of kids behind him.

Natalie peeked out from the kitchen at the explosion of noise that came from the foyer. When she saw pigtails and shoelaces, she thought about sneaking back into the kitchen, but noticed that Julie was teetering on her toes trying to keep her balance in the cyclone of kids and calf that were spinning around her.

"Hey!" She roared, startling all of the participants, including the calf, into a stunned silence. "All of you, into your snow clothes! We're taking that calf outside to Ginger."

"Awww, mom!"

"But—"

"No buts! I said git!" Natalie made a shooing motion at the kids and the calf scuttled behind Julie, butting his muzzle up against her thigh. "You too, Julie, let's get outside for a few minutes."

Julie laughed and stroked the calf's neck. "I was just going to come help you make something to eat. The guys are already outside checking on the barn."

"I've got a breakfast casserole in the oven. We'll go

check on the progress and then we can all come in and eat a late breakfast. Want some coffee first?"

"Mmmm, I'd love some." Julie glanced after the kids. "How long do we have before they're ready?"

"We've got a good thirty minutes, since those kids are masters at dawdling. This calf needs to get outside anyway. He belongs with the horse, not in the house." As if he knew they were talking about him, he pranced playfully around their legs as they wandered into the kitchen.

"I still can't believe Diego rescued this calf the way he did."

"You know, I can remember times when he couldn't rescue some of the calves. He's always been practical, but sometimes he tries too hard."

"What do you mean?" Julie asked.

"He wants to save everybody. I think that's what happened there with Patti for a bit, but he figured out quickly that by rescuing her, he'd wind up losing us. There would have been no way all of us could cohabit peacefully." Natalie poured a mug of coffee and pulled the cream out of the refrigerator. "She would yell at Aidan when he would cry. I would get pissed, Gabe was in a constant state of quiet aggression, and before long, Diego realized she had no true motherly instinct there. It took him a long time to realize it, but he really wants kids someday."

"How long did they date?"

"You know, I think it was about six months or so. It was pretty fast, and she was fun for a bit. Diego really liked her for awhile because she was a flirt and a tease

157

and she kept him on his toes a bit. Then, of course, she had really big boobs. But then reality began to set in."

"Uh oh, that doesn't sound good." Julie was surprised at how comfortable she was sitting here in the kitchen with Natalie. It was as if they'd been friends for years. She had the feeling that Natalie was easy to get along with like that. She was motherly, but fun too. She really didn't even mind the fact that the current topic of conversation was actually another woman with large breasts, and that Diego evidently had slept with her. She kind of welcomed the information, in fact.

"Ha! That's an understatement—as far as we were concerned. Well, you know how little boys can be rambunctious." Her face transformed with a motherly grin, thinking about her son. "One night, Gabe and I were out dancing and they were taking the kids for us. Aidan was a little too rowdy when she wanted quiet, and she kind of snapped. I guess she had a glass of wine on the coffee table and Aidan slipped and the glass went over. She came unglued." She shook her head in reflection. "Diego heard her scream at Aidan, and he was furious. When we got home, she was gone, and Diego and the kids were eating ice cream in the middle of the night like nothing had happened." She smiled gently. "He doesn't take well to people hurting someone he loves—whether it's physical or emotional. He's a lot like my dad. After that little incident, she didn't stand a chance."

Julie sat quietly, absorbing all that Natalie was sharing about Diego. He seemed too perfect. He could face starving predators, manage household crises, fix anything, apparently, and he was sensitive, handsome and kind. The perfect family man. What was wrong with him? What flaw did he have that she couldn't see? Maybe he was perfect. To Julie's mind, that was hard to find in this world.

"Was your dad perfect too?" Julie asked absentmindedly, idly twirling the coffee in her cup. Julie caught Natalie's speculative look and flushed. She realized belatedly how much information she just subconsciously shared with Natalie.

"Diego isn't perfect. He's wonderful, and he's talented, but he's got a mean streak a mile wide when you cross him."

"I had the feeling." Julie looked into Natalie's eyes when she said that, but her color deepened as she thought about what to say next. "After everyone left this morning, I went out and spent the rest of the night with him." Nervously, she waited to see Natalie's response.

"I know you did, honey," Natalie rested her warm hand on Julie's cool one. "It's okay." Julie's face took on an even brighter hue. "Now don't worry, he didn't kiss and tell. I guessed. So what happened?" Natalie grinned like a schoolgirl, clearly thrilled to have girl-talk with another woman her age.

"Well, when I went out there, actually, Patti was there."

"That slut?" Natalie smacked a hand against her thigh. "Don't you worry about her. She's long gone in his eyes."

Julie laughed. "She had just shown up. She said she

knew something, and I could tell how uncomfortable he was with her there. I could tell she still wanted something to do with him but he's definitely not interested in return." Her fingers strayed to the placemat on the table, and she brushed imaginary salt off the table. "She left pretty quickly. And he didn't say much about it after, either, but I could tell that she was something from the past and better left there."

"That's for sure. She was—well, you've heard enough, I suppose, about Patti. So what do you think happened in the barn last night?"

"I feel pretty confident it was arson, like they say. I just can't imagine who would want to hurt any of you guys. I don't even think Patti really had anything to do with it, now that I've met her. I mean, she just doesn't strike me as the sharpest tool in the shed."

Natalie laughed. "Nope, she's not that bright. But she is vindictive. She did a lot of things to make Diego's life hell, and she knows how to use her feminine parts to seduce other men to do things for her too. I mean, Diego put in an entire kitchen at her place before he realized how much she was using him."

"An entire kitchen? Is he nuts?" Julie laughed and shook her head. Somehow, she could see him working so hard just to please a woman that he intended to spend time with. "Tile too?" She laughed again.

"You know, actually, I think he did!" Natalie turned to look at the clock. "Let me go check on those kids. You ready to go outside?"

"Yes, I'll just get my coat and boots on and meet you at the door."

"Sounds good. Wait, just go on out. I might have to take the kids by the ear, since I don't hear them right now. That's never a good sign. Can you get this guy out there to Diego?" She nudged Snowflake's muzzle off her leg.

"Yup, I'll manage him."

Julie shook her head, amused. Diego was a pleasant surprise. She grinned, thinking about the tile Patti had to look at every day, knowing that she'd played the best man to ever walk across her doorstep for a fool.

"Come on, Snowflake, let's do this." Julie hugged the calf that seemed to be growing larger by the second. He butted her shoulder, looking for something to eat. "I know you just ate, you silly calf. Let's get outside."

Chapter Twenty Five

Ten minutes later, Julie was still trying to coax Snowflake out the door. Easier said than done, she realized when Natalie showed up, kids in tow, to help herd the recalcitrant calf out the door. He'd decided the kitchen was a far cozier place than going outside in the snow. Julie couldn't help but agree.

Once outside, the kids took off at breakneck speed for the recently destroyed barn, fascinated with the remains of the fire. The calf bounced through the snow after them. Fortunately, Gabe headed them off before they could enter the unstable building. Diego and the others followed him out to greet the kids as Julie and Natalie made their way over.

"It's not as bad as we thought," Diego said, speaking to the group.

"Do we need to tear it down before we can put the horses back in?" Natalie asked.

"We were just talking about that." He nodded at Frank. "Frank thinks we should get Jonas and a contractor out here to take a look. If we have an expert opinion that gives us the go-ahead, we'll go that way. In the meantime, we're going to build a three side shed for Ginger and Snowflake for the next few days."

"Won't hurt to pull all the gear out that wasn't destroyed, either," Frank piped up.

"You think we should get an insurance adjuster out before we do that?" Natalie checked in again.

"Jonas will help us with that. I'll give him a call."

"At least it's stopped snowing," Julie observed. "Do you think this storm is done?"

"Perhaps, but it doesn't really look like it," Natalie chimed.

"While Julie and I go check on her car and see if we can get it started or towed to Tony's, why don't you guys get started preparing a shelter for Ginger. We can just use the side of the barn that is relatively solid for now, and we'll figure out a better idea as soon as we can." He turned to Natalie. "Will you call Sheriff Bizzell and find out when he wants to meet us? Also, call Jonas and ask him to dinner."

Natalie smiled and took in the whole group with her gaze. "Of course. I'll take care of that in a bit. Before you go, though, I've made some food for all of us. John, Frank, will you come in and eat too? Stay for dinner, too."

Diego grabbed Julie's hand. leading her away from the group. "Do you want to go get your car? Or can a man hope you're planning to stay here?" He grinned cheekily at her, and she knew he was teasing.

"Can I stay forever?" She teased back.

"Of course. I happen to have some vacant space in my bed if you're interested in purchasing some property."

"Oh really? How much space is that?"
"Only enough space between the edge of the mattress and my arms, how's that sound?"

"You're a bit of a flirt, do you know that?" She grinned up at him and kissed his chin. "I happen to like that about you."

"The flirting or the space in my bed?"

"Both, actually. Want to flirt with me some more?"

"Absolutely. I'd rather take you to my bed, though." He kissed her cheek with a loud smack. "Let's get out of here so we can do this in peace, though." He put his arm around her and glanced furtively around to see who was watching. Julie giggled.

"I think Natalie knows about us, but Gabe and the kids are oblivious."

Diego sighed. "Yeah, Natalie knows. She guessed."

"She's pretty intuitive, isn't she? I bet it was nice to have a sister while you were growing up." Julie snuggled into the crook of his shoulder, and they strolled in the general direction of the driveway.

"She was a pain in the butt, growing up. She definitely made life an adventure. Without Natalie, I probably wouldn't have come back here. I just couldn't see making a life in my parents' home. Natalie was the one who suggested we turn this property into something that others could enjoy too."

"Was that hard? Deciding to come home?" Julie shivered as a gust of wind kicked up and blew under her scarf. Diego stopped and put both of his arms around her.

"It wasn't all that hard. I'd been on the road too much. I just didn't want to come home and know that my brother didn't agree with what we wanted to do, and that mom and dad were gone. They made this place happy." He tucked strands of flyaway hair behind her ear as he spoke. "It still is hard that my brother won't come back here, but he made his choice, and Natalie and her family make this place so warm and inviting."

"They sure do. I think those kids are awesome. And I'll miss Snowflake when I go."

"You had to remind me, didn't you?" The skin around his eyes seemed to tighten as he hugged her tight.

"I guess we should go check on my car, just to see if it's still there and if it will start, but I don't think it will. It was making a lot of noise on the way here the other day."

"We'll at least get it to Tony's and then we can figure it out from there. Besides, I want you to see how much space we're talkin' about here." He winked and pulled her behind him to the truck.

Chapter Twenty Six

Sheriff Bizzell knocked heavily on the front door of the Bed and Breakfast. He was late, but he didn't really care. When Natalie had called him earlier that morning, he was in the middle of an early lunch with a lady friend who had kept him up rather late the night before. He hadn't gone home after the fire; instead, he'd gone straight to her house, where he knew she'd have a bottle of bourbon waiting for him. And she did. And together they had polished it off. Instead of rushing over to Diego's, this morning, he'd gone back to bed with that lady friend for a bit. He was still a bit hungover, and she'd worn him out in other ways too.

He didn't want to deal with this fire today. He could care less about Diego Garcia and his family or his problems. Diego always took all the girls around here, well, except for Rita, his friend, but that was because Rita wasn't the cream of the crop anymore. In fact, she was getting downright old, but Jack wasn't worried about that. She was good for bourbon whenever he wanted it, and she didn't mind giving him a little of herself while she was at it. What guy would complain about that?

He was frustrated that it hadn't been a slam dunk last night with that girl staying here at Betty Lee's anyway. She was a blonde haired floozy, the kind Diego liked. But then again, she seemed smart, too, and that was a far cry from most of the girls he knew around here. But it would have been so much easier if the torn fabric on the fence had come from Julie's jacket so he could get out of this cold and go sit at Rita's with a drink in one hand and her left tit in his right. He liked that picture, and readjusted his pants as the door opened.

The redhead, Natalie stood there, with a stupid grin on her face. Jack couldn't stand her, either. She just was too happy all the time. What in the hell was there in life to be so freaking happy about anyway?

"Hello, Sheriff, come on in!"

To be polite, Jack tipped his hat, but only because his mama had been a saint and she had required that he do that for every woman. Once when he was a kid he'd forgotten and he'd about had his ear twisted off. That was the same ear that he always fiddled with whenever he was around a woman who made him uncomfortable. Like right now, for instance. He was skewered with discomfort in this room. It was packed with the whole family, including those damn kids. Didn't a body know when to keep a room quiet? Hell, he'd give his left nut just to get back to Rita and that bottle of bourbon.

Terrific. Chief Bradley was there too. Maybe he could do Jack's job for him. That would be a sight. Looks like this had been a cozy little dinner that he hadn't been invited to. Dammit, he couldn't stand these people.

"Hello, y'all." He took his hat off and stroked his ear.

"Sheriff, any news?" Diego took the lead, and Bizzell shrugged in a knee-jerk reaction.

"No news as of right now. Of course, I haven't had the chance to sit with Chief Bradley there, neither. Chief, any news from your end?"

"We believe that an accelerant was used in the far corner of the barn near the main horse stalls. It's almost a miracle you guys were able to get the horses out, actually." He nodded at Diego and Julie, who sat next to him on the loveseat near the fire.

Diego gave Julie a look that made Sheriff Bizzell want to puke. He was all lovey-dovey with that girl. He'd bet his molars that she was the reason there had been a fire anyway.

"So, an accelerant means arson, right?" Bizzell looked at Bradley, attempting to appear intelligent.

"Yes, the evidence of an accelerant would lead us to believe that this was arson." Bradley replied. "The why and who of it remains to be seen, but we can pretty safely assume that because of the color of the smoke Diego noticed early on, the odors our firefighters smelled and the heat of the fire, it was either kerosene or some sort of lighter fluid."

Bizzell bristled at the arrogance in Jonas Bradley's words. Anyone could see this was about money, and it was pretty convenient that Diego noticed the color of the smoke and all.

"That puts us back to who would want to light the barn on fire. Everybody who works around here is here tonight, and none of these people would have done such a thing, because none of us would profit from a fire in the barn." Diego was adamant that those in the room were not at fault.

Bizzell pursed his lips behind his mustache and scratched his chest. He wasn't so sure. There had to be someone at fault and he was inclined to believe that person was in this room. If Diego had a lot of insurance on the barn, that would make a lot of sense. He made a mental note to put Donna at the office on that route. She could call insurance companies and find out what Diego was up to.

"Sheriff, there was a woman who came out to visit Diego last night after the fire." This latest comment was from that blondy. Jack hiked his belt up and turned to face her. "Patti Lucero? I believe you know of her from her last encounter with Diego." Jack's eyes shifted to Diego's expression. He looked like a love-struck puppy with that sappy grin on his face.

The Sheriff reflected a moment on Patti. Ah yes, that was a fun weekend. Julie's words put things delicately. His mustache drooped on his face in frustration.

"Patti? Didn't we already put that one to rest last night?" He shook his head in irritation. He saw Julie's color rise in her face, but he didn't comment. Maybe he was putting his cart before his horse a bit. Maybe he should look at the whole situation and not just try to get back to Rita so fast. She was running low on that bottle anyway. And last week she had mentioned marriage. He probably should put some energy into this case. If Chief Bradley was convinced it was arson, then he had some legwork to do. Besides, the election was coming up. As much as he wasn't friendly with the Garcia clan, they held some clout in the community. He might be wise to put more energy into at least the appearance of keeping them on his good side.

He decided to start over. "Okay, so Patti came over last night after the fire. About what time was this?" He looked at Diego for an answer.

"She showed up pretty quickly after all of you had left. It was about two or three in the morning. I'm not entirely sure."

"And how long did she stay?"

"What does that have to do with this?" Diego appeared incensed. "She said she didn't start the fire, but she might know who did. We told her to visit with you today. She didn't do that?" Sheriff Bizzell noticed Julie put her hand on Diego's thigh. Diego seemed to calm down as soon as she touched him. Bizzell wondered what that meant. It looked like the two of them had become intimate. That added to the puzzle. If she was guilty of the fire, then this was going to raise a ruckus in the community. That might be fun.

"So if it wasn't her jacket," he said, pointing at Julie, "maybe it could be Patti's." He scratched at his ear and Julie faced him.

"Sheriff Bizzell, I know you think I had something to with this, and I am not sure why you are so convinced. I will submit to questioning if you need that to assuage your concerns." His face wrinkled, and she backtracked. "I mean, if you need me to, I'm happy to answer any questions. I did not start the fire, I'm worried that whoever did is still out there, and I think we have a strong reason to check in with Patti Lucero."

Bizzell was not keen on having this upstart tell him how to do his job. His phone jingled in his pocket and he glanced down to see Rita on the line. He sighed. "I'll check in with Patti and see where that goes. In the meantime, I expect you won't be going anywhere."

"She's staying through the holiday, Sheriff. She'll be here." Diego looked pleadingly at Julie and she nodded with a small smile.

"My car is at Tony's Garage anyway, so until that is ready, Sheriff, I have a place to stay here."

"Uh huh. Yes, well, I'll check back in the next few days." He thrust his hat back on his head as he slunk out the door and to his car.

"He already is convinced that I am the culprit." Julie sunk into the easy chair, sighing.

"Don't fret it, Jules. We'll sort it out."

Chapter Twenty Seven

Diego led Julie out by the hand, covering her eyes with his other. The snow had begun falling again, fat wet flakes that clung to eyelashes and scarves and slipped between Diego's fingers and onto Julie's cheek.

"Don't peek, now," he whispered in her ear, causing tremors of excitement to quiver along her spine. She smiled, knowing the excitement had nothing to do with whatever surprise he had waiting for her. His touch made her skin scream for more. She leaned into him just a bit, and he took the hint.

Slowly, he slid his hand down her cheek and leaned in to kiss her softly trembling lips. His kiss pressed harder into her lips and she sank deeper into the abyss of the moment. Her hips pushed against his and she sighed against his lips, feeling them curve into a smile. She started to pull back to look at him, but he held her captive in his arms, his hands creating tiny earthquakes along her back.

"Okay, you can look now," he murmured against her lips as she leaned into his chest.

As quickly as she tried to collect herself, Julie could hardly move past the vibrations on her lips, much less open her eyes to see the surprise he had planned for her.

She gasped in delight. "Oh, Diego, it's so beautiful!"

The patio glowed magically in the deepening twilight. Multi-colored lights glittered off the snow, draped around the trees, streaming across the open air, twinkling off the porch. The giant Cottonwood was glamorous in its thousands of shimmering white lights curled around the trunk and the lower limbs. The fountain had been turned on and the water flowed merrily, melting the snow as it continued to fall in fat lazy flakes.

"Diego, is there anything you can't do?" Julie laughed and turned to him, her face turned up to kiss his lips once again. He smiled back and teased her with soft pressure on her lips, then he backed away and took her hand gently, kissing her knuckles. His eyes smiled into hers as she took a deep breath, feeling suddenly light-headed. His attentions were intoxicating and she suddenly felt the urgent need to sit down before she fell down. Of course, she could use that to her advantage, knowing he'd catch her before she landed, but she opted for dignity instead.

Diego led her to the rocking chairs under the portico that were laden with quilts and cups of steaming cocoa spiked with some Irish crème. She'd be intoxicated physically as well as mentally if she wasn't careful.

He tucked her into the first chair and turned to open the door on the kiva fireplace so they could watch the fire and warm their toes as they sat in the chilly air.

"It's so beautiful," Julie murmured, savoring the comfort and warmth of her spot by the fire.

"You should see how it will look when the sun comes up, and the sky is bright blue, the snow glinting in the cool air...it's incredible," Diego agreed.

"The snow is wonderful, but I can't imagine you can get much done around here if it lingers, right?" Julie gazed at Diego's profile over the lip of her mug.

"Oh, I get enough done. I like the snow, but I've discovered I like it a bit more when there is a beautiful woman sitting next to me." He turned and winked at Julie who blushed and burrowed deeper in the colorful quilt covering her.

"Usually when it snows in Amarillo, I'm out of town. I haven't just sat and enjoyed it in years." Julie sighed.

"Oh really? Why is that?"

"I have to travel a lot for work. I'm always out of town."

Diego turned to her as he caught a wistful note in her voice.

"Do you like your job?" He asked as he pulled his chair closer to Julie's and pulled his own blanket onto his lap.

"I used to." Julie took a long sip of her cocoa and savored the chocolate on her tongue. "It was fun. It was an adventure. Ha, I sound like a commercial." She snorted at her own joke. "I enjoyed having a career for a long time, but it definitely interfered with a lot of things in my life."

Diego just nodded, not willing to interfere with the thoughts that obviously were playing havoc with Julie's mind.

"It makes it hard to build solid relationships." Julie played with the quilt on her lap.

"Boyfriends?" Diego winked at her and took a sip of

his cocoa, reminding Julie once more of the comfort of chocolate and camaraderie.

"I was married once." Julie heaved a sigh of relief at finally saying it. "I was married and so were all of my friends, and we all thought we were living life the way it was supposed to be lived." Julie struggled to work through what she wanted to share and what she wanted to keep for herself. She was beginning to understand that Diego would take whatever she was willing to give.

"I was out of town about a year ago, but decided to come home early to surprise Adam, my husband." She set her mug down and smirked, adjusting her blanket in the heat from the fire. "I surprised him alright. Him. And my best friend Sara. In my bed. On Christmas Eve."

Diego put his mug down too and shifted slightly to face Julie a bit more in his seat.

"I haven't really enjoyed the Christmas season all that much since, as I'm sure you can imagine."

"I can see this hurts you to talk about. I imagine you loved him very much."

"I did. But I think I also always knew the kind of man he was. I just turned a blind eye for a long time, thinking I could make myself better and he'd come around."

"You should know–"

"I know. I know my worth. It just took some time. I walked out and haven't looked back. I live in a single apartment with no kids, no husband, and it's just me, making it through the day every day." At that line, her eyes finally filled with tears. "I hate it. But I won't ever take that man back."

"So, do you still love him?"

"Sure! I mean, I'll always love him. He taught me much about myself and about life. But that ship has sailed."

"And do you think he still loves you?"

"I'm sure, in his own way, he still loves me. But to be honest, I'm not sure he knows how to love." She blew the steam away from the surface of the cocoa. "I probably could have seen it coming, but I was in love with being in love, and Adam was a charmer. I wanted to be in love with him." She looked up at Diego, eyes bright and tears dried. "You know?"

Diego nodded.

"Adam was the kind of guy that would take me to a concert with great tickets, but he'd always blow it." She laughed. "One time, we went to a rock concert and I told him all I wanted was to catch a drumstick because they were flying out into the audience every 3 songs or so. Sure enough, he caught one, pretty much right after I said that, but he kept it. He didn't think to give it to me because I had just mentioned it, or better, because he loved me." She snorted. "That's the kind of guy he was."

"Once I left, Adam realized that he still wanted me, even though I knew I could never trust him again. I still hear from him once in awhile, and he's upped the ante here at Christmas, which is pretty annoying. But he's also the reason why I've become so independent, so I'm grateful for that." She pulled the quilt off her shoulders, feeling warm, even though the night was cold. "I would rather get in my car and drive away and go on some

176

sort of an adventure than stay at home in my lonely little apartment and drink too much wine and have to hear the phone ring, knowing it is him and that he'll say the same things."

She sighed as she thought about the disillusionment that had come after she had walked in on Adam and Sara in her bedroom. It wasn't that she still wanted Adam, nor did she believe she still loved him, but he had taken away her fairy tale and she resented the hell out him for that. She felt sorry for him, too. It was a strange mix for her and often made her uncomfortable, which is also why she had never told Adam to just stop calling. Part of her felt like the tether kept her sane. It reminded her of who she really was and what she really wanted.

Julie stared into the fire. "Don't get me wrong, though. I don't love him anymore. He was a blip. Not necessarily a mistake, because I make different decisions in my life now because of him, but he was just a blip." She smiled out of the corner of her eyes at Diego. "He was nothing like you, that's for sure." She tugged at the blanket again, and took a sip of her drink.

She heaved a sigh and turned to Diego.

"It's not the cheating, it's not the failed marriage, it's the fact that I am 36 years old and I wanted kids. I feel cheated by that, not by his indiscretions." She blinked at him, waiting to hear criticism. Diego only nodded slightly as he stared into the fire.

"That's the way it should be. Marriage and kids, especially with a woman like you. He screwed up." Diego grinned suddenly. "Do I get to be the cowboy in the white hat?"

Julie smiled and turned back to the fire. "Wouldn't that be nice?" She murmured quietly and sank into her own thoughts of loving Diego. That *would* be nice, she decided. A man who let her be vulnerable was an even sweeter feeling.

"Wow. I could get used to this." Diego gently changed the subject, leaning back in his chair and sipping at his drink. The fire flickered off the snow and he sighed. "This is pretty nice, sitting here with beautiful company, a hot fire and a warm drink."

Julie grinned again. "Yeah, hot women and cold drinks? Isn't that what you said? I guess you like hot women and hot drinks, too?"

"Oh yeah," Diego laughed and stretched his feet closer to the fire. They sipped their cocoa in peace, as fat flakes drifted before their eyes. The lights twinkled off the snow and Julie slipped lower in her seat as the fire died. She startled herself awake with a slight snore and realized Diego was watching her.

"You sure are a sight."

She sleepily mumbled something and felt him take the mug from her hands. She settled into his embrace as he scooped her up, blanket and all and carried her back to her own room.

"I love this room" she said as he covered her with the downy coverlet.

"Sleep tight" he said, snapping the switch off to the rumble of another muffled snore. "Sweet dreams, sleeping beauty. See you in the morning."

Chapter Twenty Eight

Diego woke early and stretched his arm out, looking for Julie's soft shape. She wasn't there. He remembered putting her in her own bed last night and momentarily thought he'd lost his mind. He should have brought her here.

He remembered her dark lashes brushing the tops of her cheeks and feeling wonder at how one woman could be so lovely. His thoughts turned to her admissions of her marriage to such a schmuck. He couldn't imagine how Adam had so easily discarded her for another woman. Momentarily he wondered what it was he didn't know about Julie that could cause someone to stray. But then he realized that for some men, perfection is in imperfection. Julie was certainly perfect in his mind.

He had to work hard to put her out of his mind as he began to get ready for the day. He needed answers. Diego intended to find them. About a lot of things.

***

Diego rapped on the door of Jarrett Smith's old cabin. The lady who had lived there previously had died some years before, and the place had fallen into a sad disrepair. Diego could see attempts at fencing the front yard and sprucing up the porch, and a broom rested against the door casing, half covered in snow. Suddenly the door wrenched open. Diego had to look down to see a pair of bright blue eyes peer out of a tiny face. "Whatcha want?" The child's voice was high-pitched and cheerful in its brusque nature. He was quickly grabbed from behind and boosted onto a hip by a very young, very pregnant dark haired woman.

"May I help you?" She asked almost timidly as she looked up into Diego's face. He stepped back. The picture was all wrong. He had kind of assumed Jarrett Smith was going to be an old man who was mixed up with Patti, but this didn't fit. This girl was too young and too pregnant. Any man who would run around on this little thing with Patti deserved to be castrated and his tool flung into the ditch.

"Um," He removed his hat. "Yes, ma'am. I'm looking for Jarrett Smith. Does he live here?"

"He does, but he's out looking for work."

Diego raised his eyebrows and turned toward the door. A man looking for work in this weather, and two days before Christmas? He thought for a moment and hoped the picture was beginning to come clear. He heard Julie approach behind him, though the truck door had been muffled in the still morning air. She stamped her boots on the porch and smiled broadly at the woman before them.

"Hi, I'm Julie." Unabashed, Julie stuck her hand out and warmly shook the young woman's free hand.

"I'm Trudy Smith, Jarrett's wife. You have business

with him?" A hint of smile introduced itself at the corners of her lips, but she was terribly shy and the concern for her husband rang out like a shotgun blast.

"Excuse me, ma'am," Diego cleared his throat. "I should have introduced myself. I'm Diego Garcia, and I live just down the way there. I heard that your husband had asked about my property the other day, and, well, we've had some things happen and I just wanted to talk to him to see if he knew anything about it." Diego was as gentle as he knew how, because he felt like this was a scared doe. If she locked him out, he'd never find out what happened to his property. He certainly wasn't interested in his alternatives with Patti, nor with Sheriff Bizzell.

"Would you like to come in? We're lettin' all the heat out." Diego and Julie stepped into the modest space, and were immediately struck by how sparse everything was. Diego felt as if he had stepped back in time to another century altogether. The fireplace appeared to be the only source of heat, and there wasn't a big one burning. The woodpile to the right contained only a few dry logs.

"I'd offer you something to eat, but there isn't much, and we've a holiday comin', but you're welcome to sit a bit and chat with me." She smiled vaguely and set the boy who had answered the door on the floor.

"Oh, thank you ma'am, but we just ate anyway." Diego softened at her generosity and in his heart he knew this family was not the cause of his barn fire. They were more concerned with a roof caving in, holidays coming, and where they were going to find their next meal. They clearly needed some help, and Diego was in a position to offer it. Now he had to think about how to get it to them.

"Thank you, Mrs. Smith," Diego stood near the fire and watched the child entertain himself quietly in the corner. He noticed that there was no television, but there was an old laptop open on the kitchen table by the window.

Trudy began to fiddle with the hem of her worn t-shirt. "Jarrett didn't think he'd be long, but he wanted to run into Albuquerque to put in some applications." She looked into Julie's face. "He's been without work since we moved here a month ago." She sighed. "Money's gettin' tight."

"Oh! You just moved here?"

"When Jarrett's mama died, she left this place to him. I guess her mama before her had left it to her, but we all lived together in Marina del Rey. After he lost his job over there, we just thought we needed a new start, so we decided we'd give this place a try." She looked around sheepishly. "I think we may have put ourselves in a rougher spot." She nodded at the sagging door joints and grinned. "It's a lot of work, but it's quiet, and it's cozy, and it will be a good place to raise our children." She smoothed her hand protectively over her swollen stomach. "Y'all said you lived near?"

Diego moved to sit next to Julie on the worn sofa. "We live just on the other side of that pasture there. He gestured toward the road. "Actually, our barn caught fire the other night, and my two ranch hands had mentioned meeting Jarrett the other day. I just hoped to talk to him to see if he noticed anything odd."

"Come to think of it, we heard the fire trucks, but we didn't pay much attention. Jarrett had spent the day up on the roof trying to fix a leak, but you can imagine how awful that was. He fell off and I thought for sure he'd hurt his back. He just had to nail down some plywood so the snow wouldn't just come in. I don't know how this roof is going to hold up under all the snow since."

"Oh no! Was he injured after all?"

"Nah, he's tough. He just brushed it off."

"You said your husband went to the city in this weather?"

"Yeah, he left about an hour ago, but I don't know that he will have gotten far. This storm is really rough. We sure aren't used to this kind of snow."

"It's a hard time to try to find a job, but I'm sure he'll get something lined up. In the meantime, would you mind if I went up on your roof to shovel some of the snow off?"

Trudy was clearly uncertain, and her words said as much. "No, no, Jarrett should be home anytime, and I'd hate for you to fall or hurt yourself while up on my roof. That's very kind of you, though." Trudy stood and stretched her back. "I better get back to my chores myself, he should be home anytime."

As Diego watched the two women say goodbye, he thought about his moments of distrust of this young family. He knew he needed to meet Jarrett, though, and he had some ideas about how Jarrett could earn a living helping out at the ranch.

"Mrs. Smith, it'd be our pleasure to invite you and

your family to dinner tonight. My sister is cooking something up, and it'd sure be nice to get to know our new neighbors." He still held his hat in his hands as he spoke.

"Why, thank you, Mister Garcia. I'll ask Jarrett when he gets home."

"Oh, please do come!" Julie's smile lit the corners of the small house. "It will be so much fun." She smiled down at the boy who had brought his toy truck to show her. She knelt down in front of him. "We have some kids just your age who would love to play cars with you!" She spoke to the boy and then cocked her head to the side. "What is your name, anyway?"

"I'm Dakota." He turned proudly to his mother. "Can we go to their house, mama? Please?"

Trudy stepped forward and took him by the hand. "We'll see, darlin' boy. Let's ask your daddy when he gets home." She smiled at Diego and Julie and ushered them gently to the door.

"We'd love to see you." Diego tucked his hat securely on his head. "Say about six?"

Trudy's smile deepened. "I'll see what I can do."

Julie grasped Trudy by the wrist and looked into her eyes. "I'll set extra places for the three of you." She turned and breezed out the door as heartily as she had entered, tossing over her shoulder, "Apple pie for dessert!!" With a wave, she jumped into the truck.

"Do you think they'll come?"

"I think they might." Diego put his hand across the back of the seat as he turned to back out of the driveway. "Did you see the state of that roof? I hope this storm is done. I think I need to ask John and Frank to help me fix it this weekend."

Diego enjoyed the warmth from her tender smile. "You're a kind man, Diego."

"I don't know about kind, but I definitely know when something needs fixing." He winked at her and turned the truck in the direction of the mechanic. "It looks like quite a few things need fixing at that house. I get the sense they don't have any propane, either."

"I wonder how they've survived this storm." Julie gazed out the window at the snow piled in massive snowbanks and shook her head. "It had to have been rough on them."

"Perhaps if they come to dinner tonight we can work on some solutions. But first, let's see about your car, and then I think you just promised apple pie."

Chapter Twenty Nine

"Well, it appears that your problem with this here car was simply bad fuel!"

"What?" Julie blinked in astonishment.

"Yep. You musta put some bad gas in it, and it just clogged up that ol' fuel filter of yours, and there you have it." Tony smiled broadly, his rosy cheeks smashing his eyes to the point where they were almost closed. Julie couldn't help but be reminded of an actor from a television movie when she looked at the mechanic in front of her.

"So, it's fixed?" She was still a little off balance by the estimate. She had expected that her entire undercarriage was falling apart by the way the car had behaved on her way in, and now the Sebring was running like a champ.

"Well, it wasn't too hard to figure out. It started up when we went over there, but it kind of stuttered a bit. I bet you picked up some bad fuel somewhere along the way, and as you drove the particles just collected in that filter." He scratched the back of his neck. "It happens that way sometimes. That filter acts just like a magnet for the gunk that floats in old tanks and filling station pumps."

"I'm glad to hear it wasn't a big deal—that I won't have to replace the engine or anything."

"Nah, you just need to pay some attention to where you get your fuel. I changed out your filter for you.

"How much do I owe you?" Diego stepped up, his wallet in hand. Julie stepped forward to object, but Diego gallantly, and gently, got his way. Julie wanted to put up more of a fuss, but Diego would hear nothing out of her mouth at that moment. At first, she rejected that. She wanted to be independent. But then she warmed up as she realized that sometimes it was okay to be treated nicely. And to be treated nicely by a man like Diego? Bring it on.

Tony rescued both of them by saying, "Don't worry about it. Consider it my Christmas present to you both."

Both Julie and Diego protested, but Tony just laughed.

"Come on, Diego, you expect me to charge you over something like that when I know full and well you'll be in here with all of your rigs for the next hundred years? Let me just give y'all a little gift. It ain't much, but I 'magine bein' stranded in a strange town did a number on this lady here."

"Well, Mr.—"

"It's Tony, Miss Julie, just Tony."

"Okay, Tony. Thank you so much. I never dreamed people were as generous as what I've seen here this week. I appreciate your help."

"If you will, just get Miss Natalie to make me one of

her famous punkin pies." He grinned and rubbed his round belly. "Oh, how I love that woman's punkin pies."

"Yeah, they love you too, by the looks of it." Diego winked and put his arm around Julie's shoulder. "Thanks, Tony. I'll be seeing you soon."

***

"Hey Natalie," Diego grabbed a carrot from the pile she had just peeled. "Make enough for three more. I invited the neighbors over."

"John and Frank, too?" The news of more visitors didn't make her flinch. She lifted the lid off the pot on the stove and dumped a handful in.

"I think so, and Julie, of course."

Natalie smirked and nodded. "I already counted her, loverboy."

"Do you think she might want to hang around a little longer? I mean, Christmas is the day after tomorrow. Maybe she should stay a few days."

"Did you get her car fixed?"

"It was just bad fuel. I think she's ready to leave."

"Why don't you just ask her to stay? Swallow your pride for a minute and show her you care a little." Under her breath, she added, "or a lot."

Diego sighed heavily. "You're right." He grabbed another carrot and headed out the door. "Hey, make some apple crisp, too, wouldja? Oh, and Tony wants one of your famous 'punkin' pies as payment for the car. He didn't even charge us."

Natalie tossed the spoon on the counter and put her hands on her hips. "Diego. How much do you seriously expect me to cook today?"

Diego did an about face and sidled up to her, putting his arm around her shoulder. "I promise I'll come help. Let me just go find Julie and convince her to stay and then I'll be back in here. I'll peel potatoes. Or boil pumpkins. Whatever you want. Okay, sis?"

"Men. You're all alike." Natalie batted his ribs with the back of her hand and turned back to the stove. "Fine. I expect you to peel potatoes *and* boil pumpkins. It sounds like we'll need a lot of them."

***

Diego hooked his left thumb in the belt loop of his jeans and leaned back against the hood of the truck. Snow swirled around the black cowboy hat that hung low over his brow, but he didn't notice it. He watched Julie bend to pet the dogs as they bounced around her knees, her laughter floating in the still air. He smiled as Tater jumped and Julie stepped back to gain her balance. She pushed him down with her knee and laughed again, then playfully rubbed the scruff of his neck, crooning endearments all the while.

Diego couldn't imagine watching her leave the next day. He wished her car wasn't fixed, and he wanted to wrap her in his arms and hold onto her until she realized the same feelings he felt. He loved her completely and without regret. He couldn't quite imagine how quickly it had come on him, but he knew it to be true. She was smart, funny, strong and confident, and she fit in his life just right. She filled in all the holes that he had been trying desperately to fill until he had met her, but she didn't know it. He knew he had to tell her.

He pulled on a loose thread on the front of his canvas Carhartt jacket, thinking. He knew Julie was as skittish as a green filly and if he pushed too hard, she'd run.

"Diego! Come over here!" Her smile lit the afternoon, and his knees went weak. "What has she done to me?" The dogs went nuts as they saw him coming, bouncing around him and jumping up on him.

"Maybe one of these days I should teach these guys not to jump." He rubbed Shadow's ears and smiled up at Julie.

"That would be a good thing, I think." Her giggle slammed into Diego and he felt his stomach drop into his pants. She just couldn't leave.

"Julie, I—"

The thought of facing the next day without her made it hard for him to breathe. He was afraid of what she would say if he pushed her to stay, and he was afraid of what she wouldn't say if he didn't. He shook his head then put his arm around her back, pushing her hair out of her face with his other hand. She leaned into him and he grinned down into her face. "You fit just like you were meant to be right here in my arms like this."

Julie smiled up at him, her head cradled between his arms, his hand holding her hair out of her face. He could see her contentment and hoped she would let it radiate through her, let it signal her that she was warm and safe and, mostly, tell her that she wanted to stay.

"I love being with you, Diego." He watched her hesitate. He knew the thoughts she was torn between. "I had actually kind of hoped my car wouldn't be ready so soon."

"Don't let your car make you leave. Just stay through the holiday."

"I've already imposed so much."

"You take up less space than that calf."

"I'm glad to hear that, since he's already twice as big as Shadow over there."

"Do you have a Christmas tree in your apartment?"

"No, I don't." She rubbed her face against his chest and Diego thought he probably was never going to recover.

"Do you have to work the day after?"

"No, I don't."

"Do you have food in your pantry?"

He watched her scrunch up her face as she thought. "Umm…no. I don't."

"Then you have no reason to go! Stay here!"

"You say that to all the girls."

"Actually, only you."

"And Patti?"

"She came on to me. I never actually asked her to stay."

"What will Natalie think?"

"Natalie will be over the moon."

"Let me think about it."

"Take your time. We can talk about you leaving after we spend tomorrow celebrating life."

"I don't want to leave," she whispered.

"Then don't leave. Stay here." He gazed back into her eyes, searching for her answer as he leaned closer to kiss her. His lips pressed deeply into hers and her hips sank against him, her body giving in to his passion. When the kiss broke, the passion hung on the air.

"Don't leave. Stay. Stay here with me," Diego pleaded.

"Diego," Julie sighed and looked away. "I don't know how to stay."

Her vulnerability touched him. Humor was his response.

"It's easy. You put your keys in my pocket and I never give them back to you." He grinned again and gently moved the strand of hair that wisped into her face.

Julie smiled back and hugged him tighter.

"I wish it were that easy." She sighed. He wrapped his arms more tightly around her shoulders, heaving a sigh of his own.

He gazed earnestly down at Julie. "Why can't it be that way? Why do we always have to do what's right, rather than what feels good?" Diego took a small step back. "Really, Julie, why shouldn't we be together?"

"I guess because I have my life back there, and you have yours here..." She trailed off, not making a very solid case, even to her own ears.

"I'm going to have to change your mind, I see." Diego grabbed her by the waist and hoisted her over his shoulder, her giggle giving him permission. "Right after I make love to you."

Chapter Thirty

Jarrett was an inch or so taller than Diego, skinny as a scarecrow, and had laughing gray eyes and crow's feet that had begun to creep into his hairline. One look at him, and Julie knew he had nothing to do with the fire to Diego's barn. Jarrett and Trudy had shown up promptly at six o'clock, and Dakota's hair had been spit-shined and combed neatly. Natalie's mother-hen instinct had them seated at the table within minutes and dinner was served.

The kids stole Dakota away and the three of them set up shop at the kid's table nearest the kitchen. The adults settled in with the ease of a cold Christmas evening wrapped in the warmth of the cozy dining room, the fire crackling and spitting in the living room next to them.

Frank broke the silence about the barn fire, though conversation had been lively and gregarious for over an hour. "Do you know who set fire to the barn out back?"

Trudy's eyes grew big in her face and Natalie rushed in.

"We had a fire and it appears to have been set deliberately. We just don't know who would have done such a thing."

Trudy looked down at her plate and Jarrett grimaced. "I heard the sirens and saw the barn on my way to the city today. I don't know who set it."

"But we did have a weird visit from a woman who was awfully interested in getting Jarrett to do some side jobs for her." Trudy clearly was not a fan of the woman she was speaking about. Her eyes were large in her face and two matching red blotches filled her cheeks. "I didn't like the looks of her, though, so I put my foot down and Jarrett said no."

"Well, that *is* kind of how it happened." Jarrett blushed also. "She was a little forward and didn't really seem to respect that I was wearing a wedding ring and my wife was sitting in the same room with us."

"Patti." Six voices piped up together and the kids looked up from their apple crisp and ice cream, finally noticing that the adults were still there.

"Come to think of it, I do think that was her name." Trudy dropped her fork on her plate and wiped her lips with her napkin. "Do you all know her pretty well?"

"She's been here a time or two."

"She's not our favorite person. She told me she knew who set it, but she kind of hinted, Jarrett, that it might have been you."

Jarrett could have become offended at the way that

conversation developed, but his manners were deeply ingrained and he paused thoughtfully for a moment before responding. "I suppose I can see how you might have thought that. And us being new here and all, and suddenly a fire crops up, you probably didn't know what to think. But I swear to you, I had nothing to do with it." Trudy put her hand on his thigh as his voice trembled. "I hope to have my own set up one day, and have some horses and cattle, but I'd never do it the wrong way. I couldn't live with myself if I had."

Julie felt the tension that had begun to rise in Jarrett and she rushed to ease it. "We found a piece of a black jacket on the fence. We think it might be hers, but we haven't been able to find out. The Sheriff said he'd talk to her."

"She was wearing a black jacket when she came to visit the other day." Trudy's voice was suddenly firm and strong, as if the mystery of the fire and the tendered accusation had built her backbone. "I know, because I admired it when she came inside. She was rather condescending when she told me I'd never be able to afford one like it."

"That's definitely Patti." Gabe's eyes spit fire. "I cannot abide that woman."

"Don't mind him, Trudy. Patti did the same thing to me and Gabe when we first met. She just tries to find weaknesses." Natalie patted Gabe's hand.

"I hate to say it, but all of us are thinking the same thing." Diego sighed and wiped his lips with his napkin. "She has been a thorn in my side for too long, and I know it is my fault she is still around."

"Now, you can't blame yourself for her behaviors just because it didn't work out for the two of you!" Frank was gruff, but firm. "Women like that just don't take rejection well. You haven't had enough years on this earth to have known it when you met her, but now you do. You'll just have to let the law manage this."

John snorted into his napkin. "The law? That Sheriff is about as worthless as a wooden nickel."

"But he is the law. He will do what's right, if he wants to keep his job. Diego knows too many people for a man like that to get away with chasing skirts and letting a barn burn down." Frank took another bite of potatoes. "Mm-mmm, Natalie. You sure do know how to put together a dinner spread."

"Frank is right. And Jonas has a handle on this too." Diego pushed his chair back and stood up. "I'm going to open another bottle of wine. Any takers?"

***

The Christmas celebration that began as dinner turned into a pleasant party of games and wine and children's laughter. The heavy conversation of earlier had turned into thoughts of spring and a possible partnership for Diego, Jarrett, Frank and John, running cattle along some of Frank's old trade routes. Diego's rodeo connections would help them to make sales, and with the use of several of Diego's bulls, they were planning to raise up quite a herd, while sharing the land.

"In the meantime, though, we need to get a roof on your house and find you some work. How about you help raise up a new barn with us this week and I'll pay your wages?" Diego felt beneficent and was shy to have so much abundance, but he had worked hard over the years to make it happen for himself.

"I appreciate that, sir."

"Jarrett, please, don't ever call me that again. If we are going to be partners, we're equals."

"Besides, you'll give him a big head." Frank grumbled into a grin.

"He already has a big ego." Natalie quipped from her corner of the sofa where she sat with her feet in Gabe's lap. "He sure doesn't need titles, too."

"Well, we sure appreciate your hospitality, but we'd better be heading out." Trudy yawned in the corner as Jarrett spoke, and Dakota snored in response from her lap. "I look forward to working with you all. I feel very lucky to have taken a risk by moving here, even if the house is falling apart in places."

"We can help you with all of that." Diego spoke kindly to a man who had been a stranger and a suspect just hours before. "Thanks for coming over, and I am glad to know we have good neighbors once again."

"We best be headin' out too." Frank stood and pulled his jacket tight, and John put his hat on his head.

"Nat, thanks for dinner! As always, it was a pleasure." John shook Gabe's hand and they all headed out.

"Merry Christmas!"

As Natalie and Gabe closed up the house, Diego whispered his desire in her ear. Julie blushed but nodded that she longed for him too. "Meet me in my house." Diego kissed her and went out to check on the calf and Ginger.

"Don't be long, Diego, I'm so tired I might just be asleep as soon as I set foot in that room." She fairly ran up the stairs to grab some things to take out to Diego's, her smile stretched across her face.

Chapter Thirty One

She couldn't imagine living in her apartment after having spent the last few days in the glorious space of the ranch. She couldn't imagine going back to solitude after the welcome noise and love of the family that lived here. And she couldn't imagine living her life without the man who now filled it. She watched him covertly as he stood looking out the picture windows that faced the sunrise.

The blue mountains wavered in the distance, framing him in the vista while frozen droplets of snow hung timelessly in the sunrise. Julie had never seen such a beautiful sight in her life. She felt like she could reach out and touch the crags, but New Mexico distances deceived the eye. She knew they were miles away, more miles than she could walk in a day. She did reach out and touch him. She stroked his shoulder and turned to meet her.

"How do I tell you what you mean to me after just such a short time?"

"If you feel remotely like I do, you don't have to."

Diego kissed the hand that rested on his tricep and she looked up at him.

"How do I convince you to let me in?"

"You are in." Julie took a step back and looked up at him questioningly. "I feel the same about you."

"Can we make it work through the distance?"

"I don't know."

She stood there, her hair a cloud, and she knew a fright, and she didn't care. She longed to stay, but she just couldn't see how to practically do it. She had an apartment to manage. Her things were there. And besides, it had been less than a week!

"You belong here. You were made for this place. You were made for loving me."

"That sounds like a song." She wanted to laugh, but she knew he wasn't being funny. He was dead serious.

She belonged here. On some level, she knew she was made to be in this house with him and with his family. She wanted him to tease and play, but she knew this was serious. And she knew she had to leave.

"I can be patient." He set his coffee down and turned to her. "You won't be that far away."

"I think we need more time to sort this out, so I really appreciate that."

"Do we always have to be so practical?" His face

softened and she leaned into him, grateful the tension had receded. The sex was out of sight, and she would miss that, but she also was excited to know that he wasn't going to be out of her life forever. She could return. He could visit. They could make it work.

"You're beautiful," he drawled.

"So are you." She let her robe slip off one shoulder flirtatiously. She grinned as Diego drew in a sharp breath and she followed his eyes as they shot fire into her belly. They fell into each other's arms, famished for one another. Julie's lips sought his as he twisted handfuls of her hair in his fist, pulling her head back to meet his, their passion sparking into flame as their tongues and lips stroked in turn.

Julie slid her arms up his back and across his shoulders, then grasped his face in her hands. His skin was like fire, and he wrapped his arms tightly across her shoulder blades, squeezing her body as close to his as he could.

"I can't wait to have you," Diego murmured against Julie's neck as he lapped up her energy, making her knees weak.

"I'm right here," Julie whispered, her hands sliding down his back to his hips, dragging him closer to her, her pelvis urgently pushing against the erection she felt pressing into her belly.

Diego pushed her back and sucked in a deep breath. "Let me look at you."

The firelight flickered over her now bared shoulders and she opened the robe further, letting it V down the front. Her breasts rose and fell heavily, and her eyelids had slitted as she looked at the man she was falling deeply, helplessly in love with.

Diego growled and grabbed her again, flipping off the robe and letting it drop to the floor. He kissed her deeply and drugged them both with his desire. Julie's hands groped and ripped at his shirt, wanting, needing his skin against hers. She couldn't wait any longer and wrapped her long legs around his waist, pushing him back onto the sofa, where his hands moved along her body, followed by his tongue, stroking and suckling her golden skin.

"I want you," Julie gasped.

"Oh baby, I need you." Diego fumbled with his pants and finally flipped her over on her back so he was above her. He knelt again, more slowly this time. She smiled up at him, encouraging him to complete the movement. She was rewarded with tiny, slow, determined kisses on her eyes, her nose, her cheeks and when he slid his hand down to the soft moist center, she almost lost her mind.

She pulled in a deep breath and pushed her hips up. He took the hint and thrust into her, and they both sighed in relief. The cold night air was suddenly humid and warm, and she heard nothing but his breath in her ear as they made love. His motions became more urgent and suddenly Julie cried out, wrapping her hands more tightly around his back, scraping her nails down his shoulders. Diego shuddered and the two came together, their climax exploding through the early morning air.

He stroked her hair back and smiled down on her

sweat-slicked face.

"Merry Christmas, Julie."

"Merry Christmas, Diego."

Chapter Thirty Two

Sheriff Bizzell was pissed that it was Christmas and that Rita wasn't still in bed keeping him warm. He had a message on his phone from Diego already this morning. Damn that man, didn't he recognize a holiday?

"Buzz, your breakfast is ready." Rita was a sweetheart, even if she was getting old, and she sure did care about him.

"I'll be right there, woman!" He fumbled for his pants and pulled them over his skinny thighs. "It is Christmas, and she is making me breakfast." He mumbled to himself as he swiped a tired hand over a tired face.

Fifty three years old and he felt like he was a hundred. Where had the time gone? Where had his life gone? He used to be so excited to wear the badge, and he looked forward to every day as if it were the adventure he believed it to be.

Bizzell stood and swayed. He'd had too much to drink last night, and he'd fallen asleep in Rita's arms before he'd even gotten her blouse off. Damn. He *was* getting old.

The smell of bacon lured him, and the scent of coffee got him moving. He threw a tshirt on and a pair of socks, and stepped into the bathroom to brush his teeth. His eyes were dilated and he felt numb, but the food smelled like something he wanted, and fast.

He made his way into the kitchen and swatted Rita on the behind. "Hey good lookin'."

Rita giggled like a schoolgirl and turned to kiss his cheek.

"After breakfast you should shave, and then you can open your gift."

"Rita, I told you, I don't want you spendin' your money on me. I ain't no man you should set your heart by."

"You keep saying that, but you keep showing up, Buzz. Make up your mind, and make it up quick. I'm tired of Christmases where you wake up and make me love you again. This has been going on for far too long, and we are far too old for you to be messing with me." Rita's sweet smile had turned to a grim portrait of a woman tired of waiting.

Bizzell's mouth dropped open as he watched her

pick up her coffee mug and stalk out of the kitchen. She had never spoken to him like that before. He was surprised. He kind of liked it.

She burst back into the room and tossed a gaily wrapped gift festooned with a bow on the table next to his plate. Then she turned, and without a word, went upstairs to start the shower.

Bizzell slowly closed his mouth as he picked up the package and tried to figure out where the ribbon should be pulled. He'd never given much thought to gifts, but he enjoyed Rita, and they always had a good time together, with or without the bourbon.

It made him kind of sad to see the photo that Rita had lovingly had framed. Earlier that summer the two had gone to Giggling Springs in Jemez for a day of hot baths and cold river jumping. That had been a lot of fun. Bathing in the mineral water made the body feel good, but it also wasn't good to drink booze, so she had insisted they lay off and just drink coconut water. Buzz drinking coconut water. He smirked at that memory. Never in his life...She did other things for him too, not just sweet gifts and food. She washed and pressed his uniform, and she fed his dog when he would go out of town. She planted flowers in his front yard. She was a good girl. He definitely didn't appreciate her enough.

He felt tenderness wash over him, and realized he was an ass. He wanted to be better. He wanted to do better. He grabbed a slab of bacon, crammed it in his mouth and went upstairs to join Rita in the shower. Hopefully she'd forgive him. Then he'd go take care of Diego and that fire. He knew what he needed to do.

There was no time like the present to start making things right.

Chapter Thirty Three

Christmas at Betty Lee's was an affair to remember, with kids squealing over the gifts they unwrapped, trading, playing, and sharing their spoils. They wanted to invite Dakota over until Gabe laughingly talked them into some hot breakfast first, reminding them that Dakota was having his own Christmas at his house.

Diego was edgy, but his smile was easy. He was dreading the moment Julie would announce that her things were packed and she was heading out. Julie was in a similar state. She would watch Diego until he would turn his head to look at her, then she'd find something else to occupy her attention. She was dreading the thought of climbing into that cold car to head home.

Natalie watched all of this with fascination. She was concerned that the two of them were both feeling the same thing, but they weren't willing to come clean about it. There was nothing she could do, if Diego and Julie wouldn't do it themselves. She itched to say something, but remembered that the last time she had, Patti had practically moved in.

But Julie was a very different girl, and Diego knew what devastation Patti had wrought. He was smarter and yet, he was weak when it came to Julie. Natalie could see that something was going to give pretty soon between the two of them, and she hoped it would result in the best ending possible.

The doorbell was unexpected, but Diego leapt to his feet as if he'd been expecting it.

"Sheriff! So glad you could make it. We were just about to eat. You hungry?"

"Well, thanks, Diego, but I just ate." He was contrite and polite, and he tipped his hat at Julie and Natalie, and smiled at the kids. "I just dropped by to let you know that I have arrested Patti Lucero on the suspicion of setting fire to your barn. I've included bodily harm, since Miss Julie here could have been hurt as she tried to get the horses out. I believe the charges will stick, as her jacket has also been found, and it does have a corresponding tear on the left shoulder."

Cheers erupted as the news sunk in around the room.

"Sheriff, thank you so much." Julie smiled her warmest smile and the Sheriff blushed.

"I should have paid more attention the other night to the things you said, ma'am, and for that I apologize."

"No need, Sheriff. You've taken care of it. Now Diego can rebuild and move forward."

"Well, I need to be getting back to Rita. She's got dinner in the oven and she and I have some things to talk about. Diego, I hope we can sit down for a beer sometime soon and sort things out as friends."

"I look forward to that, Sheriff."

Chapter Thirty Four

The moment had come. Julie had struggled with whether to stay longer, or to make the break happen now that the excitement had passed, the mystery of the fire was solved, and the kids were distracted. She had gone upstairs and sat on the spacious bed, looking around the gorgeous room, wishing for all she had that she could remain here. When she went downstairs, the look on Diego's face told her she was making a mistake, but she was stubborn and made it anyway.

"I'll miss you so much, Diego." She closed the space again and pressed her face to his chest.

"Julie—"

He sighed deeply and dropped his chin. "I know you have to go. I wish it were different." He rested his cheek on the top of her head. "Do you think you'll ever come back this way?"

Julie pulled back and gazed up at him again. "Are you asking me to?" Her eyes glistened with tears, but she held them tightly so he would not see them fall.

"Well, little darlin', if you don't, I might have to steal you."

They laughed companionably together, but the sadness quickly stole the humor. Julie sniffed and took a step back. She had to explain, but knew it wouldn't be enough for this man who demanded her heart and her soul, and she ached to give them both to him. Her fears that she would never be enough, never be what he needed, forced her words out.

"Diego, I have to go. I have to be happy alone before I can be happy with you, and I know that I have some things in my life that I have to take care of." She sighed again and looked up at his whiskered face. He pleaded with her, his eyes looking into her soul. "My job, my apartment, the way I know my life looks—it's not the best, but it's mine."

"Julie, I have never felt this way about anyone. I admit that it's fast, but I can't help it. You're so interesting and you captivate me. I love you more than my own self."

"Diego, I care for you too. I think you are amazing,

and thoughtful, and wonderful, but I have to go back. I have to see if I can do this for once without waking up and thinking that I am only a piece of who I used to be."

"But you don't love me." Diego angrily ran a hand through his dark hair and turned away.

"No, Diego, that's not—" Julie reached for his arm, then let her hand drop as she realized how much she had hurt him, not with her words, but with her lack of them. To say what her heart sung would be trite and insincere now that he had turned away. With tears in her eyes, Julie quietly picked up her purse and moved to the door. Her hand on the knob, she turned one last time to look at him, but saw only the set of his shoulders and heard only the silence in the room. The first traitorous tear slid down her cheek and she slipped out of the room, knowing in her heart that she had just made the most treacherous mistake of her life. She never saw Diego's glassy eyes, mirroring her own, his own anguish streaking across his face.

Chapter Thirty Five

Julie pulled into the infamous Wal-Mart parking lot, and parked her car in a space near where she had recently been buried by the snowplow. She sat for a moment, reflecting on her last moments with Diego. In her mind she once again watched his house recede in her rearview mirror, knowing that she was doing the practical thing, but in her heart, she was ripping apart.

"I'll never see him again," she whispered, and put her face in her hands. Tears raced down her face and dripped onto her scarf. Her hands mopped at the tracks, but her treacherous eyes had sprung a leak and she was drowning in her own sorrow.

She began to sob, her shoulders wracked with anguish, and no one to comfort her. She glanced in the rearview mirror and saw her red-rimmed eyes soaked in salty tears. She laughed morbidly.

"Why do I even bother with makeup?" She swiped at the droplets that began to slow as she forced herself to put a lighter expression on her face. She clenched the scarf and tried to soak up the tears that would freeze if she stepped out of the warm car.

One tear slowly slid down along her fingers as she breathed quietly, images of Diego over the past few days looming large and long in her mind's eye.

She knew she was right. A deep breath in. She could never be the right woman for Diego if she couldn't figure out what was right and wrong in her own life. Deep breath out. She hoped the drive home would help clear some of the mud out of her mind. Surrendered intake of air. Anguished expel. She turned the key and faced the car eastward, toward a place she called home, even though her real home suddenly seemed to lay behind her. Her smile sadly replaced the tears and she flicked the radio on in a desperate attempt at distraction.

***

Diego slammed the door of his truck shut and sat still for a moment, his eyes unfocused, his thoughts on the woman who had driven out of his life, possibly forever. His eyes snapped shut and he hit the steering wheel with his hand. "Why'd she have to go?" He felt anger, dismay, disappointment, and the keenest sense that he just hadn't done enough to make her stay. He turned the key and put the truck in drive. He planned to distract himself with errands in the city, but that would take him further in the opposite direction of the woman he knew he was in love with.

His gaze flicked to the gas gauge and he grunted at the fuel gauge that signaled full.

"I'm going to get her." He threw the truck in gear, peeled out of the driveway and headed his truck east to Amarillo.

***

Julie moped about her apartment, picking books off the bookshelf and tossing most of them into a copy paper box. She shook her head as she gazed at the shelf full of thousand plus page novels she had bought last summer, planning to read when she got around to it. She never got around to it. Into the box they went.

"I can't stand this apartment anymore, she grumbled. "I hate all of this stuff. I can't even think straight with all of the books and shoes I have in here." She wandered into her closet and started hauling shoeboxes out, stringing jeans and sweaters along the way as she went. She threw her ratty old bathrobe across the bed and sighed.

"That's it. I'm getting rid of all of this crap." She moved into the kitchen and pulled out a garbage bag to load up all of the clothes and shoes that she no longer wore. The phone rang just as she crawled into the recesses of her closet to get the forgotten shoes that had collected dust in the last year. "Oh geez." She muttered as she backed out of the closet and into a pair of legs.

Julie screamed and scrambled forward, turning at the same time.

A nervous snicker sounded from above as Julie pushed to her feet.

"Adam, what the hell are you doing here? And how did you get in?" She slicked her hair out of her face and started to rearrange the ponytail that had shifted in her panicked escape back into the closet. The phone continued to ring and Julie's heart raced as she tried to compose herself and make sense of what was going on in her apartment. The clothes and shoes that littered her floor, bed, and vanity didn't help matters. And why the hell was this bastard in her bedroom, much less her apartment? Her face flushed and anger swelled in her chest. It felt really good. She balled her fists and glanced down. Wow. That felt even better. When had she gotten this good and mad?

Adam had the decency to blush and look at his feet as Julie sucked air into her lungs.

"I missed you. I haven't heard from you in awhile, so I came over to check on you."

"How did you even find my apartment? And when was the last time you heard from me, anyway? You call me—remember? Get out of my bedroom." Angrily, she shooed him out in front of her and solidly closed the door behind her as she followed him into the living room.

"Jules," He stopped and turned to face her, catching

her arms in his hands. Julie pulled back, nervous to be so close to this man who had abused her love. She looked at him now and saw none of Diego. In her mind that man rose up to eclipse the one standing before her. She shrugged her arms free of his grasp and opened the front door.

"You need to go. Now."

"But Jules—"

"No. I'm through. This has been over for a long time. You screwed up—remember? You cheated on me. You are the one who calls me all the time. And I don't answer for a reason! It's got to stop." Her chest heaved and she pointed at the hallway. "Out. Leave."

"But—"

"No. I'm in love with someone else."

"Julie, I'm not going anywhere. You married me because you loved me once, and I mean to have you back." Adam's voice rose to a shrill pitch and Julie looked at him in amazement, still holding the doorknob of the open door.

"You what?" She shook her head in amazement, not sensing the potential danger. "You cheated on me! We're divorced—remember? You blew it, Adam, not me. And honestly, I'm glad you did. I've met someone who gives me more emotional contentment and fulfillment than you could dream of."

Adam's face grew red, and a pulse began to throb in his forehead.

Julie went on, beginning to notice the danger signs, but unable to stop herself.

"In fact, he has more love in his little finger than you

have in your whole body! Go sleep with Sarah, or with twenty women, if that's what you want. I don't want you in my life anymore! Ever! We're through!" Her voice had risen perceptibly itself, her anger forcing the words to come out in clipped, rationed chunks. She saw Adam's fist raised, and flinched, waiting for the blow to land on her cheek. It never came. The crash she heard instead came seconds after a giant blur in black hurtled past her, removing Adam from her sight.

"Diego! What are you doing here?" Julie gasped in shock and delight coursed through her body, even as she watched the two men wrestle on the floor before her. She edged around the sofa and the coffee table tipped toward her as Adam placed a punch to Diego's ribs.

"Diego!" Julie shrieked his name, and his head jerked up at the sound of her voice. Adam got another lucky punch in at that moment, so Julie clapped her hand over her mouth and watched as Diego effectively hog-tied Adam with the afghan that once rested on the edge of the sofa.

"I had to come find you!" Diego gasped out as he grabbed Adam's right arm and pinned it beneath him. "I couldn't stop thinking about you." He glanced up at her as he pushed Adam's thrashing body into the sofa. Adam finally sank down, his energy spent against the stronger and taller man who pressed his body weight against him.

"Julie" Adam sobbed. "Get this heathen off of me!"

"No." Julie beamed at Diego, and forgot about Adam as she took a step closer.

"Darling, as much as I'd like to kiss you right now, do you think you might want to call the police, or is this guy worth it?" Diego grinned into Julie's shining face and thought his heart might just fall through the floor, especially now that the danger had been averted.

"Oh, I guess...Let him go?" Julie cocked her head at Diego, unsure whether Adam was going to be a threat now that he was subdued or not. Diego looked at Julie calmly and wiped the tiny trace of blood that was on the corner of his mouth from the shot that Adam had gotten through.

"Probably a good idea. You better hit the road, brother. You won't have another chance for us to be so nice. She kicked you out. You need to go. For good." Diego's eyes took on the threat of stormclouds and promised to be just as violent.

Adam rolled over and nodded his head. "I see. Do you think you might untie me?" Diego glanced at Julie again, and then unwound the blanket he had used to tie Adam's hands together. Once free, Adam smoothed his hair and rolled to his knees, then his shoulders heaved as if he was going to throw up.

"Don't you dare do that on my living room carpet!" Julie glared at him, daring him to puke on her antique oriental rug.

"I'm leaving. I'm leaving." Adam supplicated with his hands out towards her. "Are you sure, Julie? I still love you so much." His eyes filled with tears, but Julie was unmoved. Diego snorted. He was unimpressed with Julie's former taste in men.

"After all that you did? After this?" She shook her

head and took a step closer to where Diego stood. "No. You need to leave." She smiled up at Diego and lovingly put a hand on his chest. "This is where I belong," she murmured softly, gazing into the blue eyes that softened as they gazed into hers.

"Did you really mean what you said? About meeting someone you loved?" Adam was forgotten and the two gazed at each other raptly. Julie nodded, pressing her hips into his. "Oh, Julie, after you left, I realized that my life was empty without you. I don't always know what I need to do, or where I need to be, but when I jumped in my truck, I knew I was headed after you. I had plenty of time to reflect and think on the drive here, and I realized that I'm the best when I'm with you. I'm grounded. I'm focused. You ground me. You make me more of a man than I've ever been."

A silent tear rolled off her cheekbone and his finger caught it. "Don't cry, love. I'll leave, if that's what you need, but I had to tell you how I felt. I couldn't let you leave me without knowing what I feel for you." Through her tears, Julie began to smile.

"I am so sorry, Diego. I am so sorry I ever left. I thought I had to come back and figure out who I really was, but I knew myself all along. I just needed you." She gazed into his blue eyes, happy to be looking at him once again. "You are the piece I need in my life. You are the best thing that has ever happened to me." Julie's eyes filled with tears as she looked at him, sure he would reject her at the last minute. He gazed softly into her eyes and brushed her hair away from her cheek.

"Don't cry, Jules. Just come home with me now."

She threw her body against his and wrapped her arms around his neck as he collected her in his arms.

"Do you think we could be in love like this forever?" She murmured into his neck.

"I'm pretty willing to find out," he whispered back.

"Then let's not go home yet, let's go see whose bed is better. Yours, or mine." She grinned wickedly and he kicked the door shut, carrying her toward a new life.